MW01680324

Murder With A View

Copyright © 2009 K.A. Neely

ISBN 978-1-60145-791-2

All rights reserved. No part of this publication may be reproduced, stored in a retrieval system, or transmitted in any form or by any means, electronic, mechanical, recording or otherwise, without the prior written permission of the author.

Printed in the United States of America.

The characters and events in this book are fictitious. Any similarity to real persons, living or dead, is coincidental and not intended by the author.

PawsForLoveMystery.com
rickandkim1231@gmail.com

Murder With A View

K.A. Neely

A Paws For Love Mystery

For my husband,
Rick,
my knight in shining armor.

Acknowledgements

I am thankful my Lord and Savior has blessed me with a modicum of writing ability and also with friends, and family who have given me encouragement and love along the way. To my best friend and cohort, Jayme, who gave me the inspiration for the story; to Katie, for her unfailing belief in my potential; and to the real-life Cooper and all my pets for years of love. Thanks, also, to my readers, to whom I give a little of myself. May you find a smile along the way.

"Be still, and know that I am God" Psalm 46:10

CHAPTER 1

Saturday, October 5

The Fall Fest Ball appeared to have been successful although the handful of members still left at Harbor View Yacht Club were trapped for now because of the storm surge. We were all jitterbugging and line dancing, trying to ignore the frenetic rhythm of the rain and wind. Except for the weather problem, everything had gone as planned and I was thankful. The other committee members and I had worked hard to make this night an evening to remember, but the weather had made the event perhaps *too* memorable for the thirty-some people still left in the building. The loud music could not mask the crashing thunder of the storm passing overhead.

The lights began to flicker and a macabre feeling tingled down my back. The lights went out, thunder rolled, and a scream vibrated the air. Then everything went silent and dark. The only illumination came from the decorative oil lamp centerpieces on the tables.

Barbara Voorhees, wife of a local jewelry storeowner, came rushing down the pitch-black hallway, feeling her way along the walls. "Quick, someone help me," she cried. "It's Emile…It's my husband…I think he's…I think he's dead."

"Call 9-1-1," someone shouted.

"The landlines are down," cried another voice.

"The emergency services won't be able to get through. The road's flooded," someone else called out.

Chaos overtook the small crowd. People frantically fumbled for their cell phones, but to no avail. This was an area prone to signal block-out. Worse yet, no electricity foretold an evening continuing into morning.

With emergency room precision, Susan Fairfield, a doctor at Newport General, grabbed an oil lamp from one of the centerpieces and double-timed it in the direction of Barbara's voice. I followed in hot pursuit.

"Take me to him," she said. Barbara Voorhees fumbled her way back to where she had left her husband. He was lying on a small leather couch in the head chef's office. His legs were bent toward his chest. His back facing us, a knife protruded from it at an unnatural angle. Barbara stood at the doorway, motionless, showing no signs of concern or emotion. All I could do was put my arm over her shoulder for comfort and support.

Susan set her lamp on a small table near the body, but more shadows than light bathed the scene. She leaned over and placed two fingers on Emile's neck, resting them for a moment. I watched the dead man's wife studying the doctor's actions. She seemed distant and detached. I squeezed her shoulder tighter, thinking she had to be in shock.

While we waited for Susan to speak, my instinct was to shake Emile and tell him this wasn't funny. I had interviewed witnesses of nursing home abuse and dog fighting, but I had never been privy to the actual crime scene. It took us all a moment to understand and recognize the inevitable. After seconds that seemed like minutes, Susan turned to me and quietly stated what we both knew. "This was murder. Did anyone reach 9-1-1 yet?"

My heart began pounding faster. My mind flipped back to a month ago and the last time my heart had beat at such a rhythm. I was on a freelance investigative story. It revolved around murder of a different sort: the horror of puppy mills. I also owned a pet store, so I understood, perhaps better than others, the lengths people would go to to make a buck at the expense of life. I confronted evil firsthand as I scooped poop in those dreadful conditions. Life is full of atrocities, and here lying before me on the couch was one more. I wondered if Barbara Voorhees, whom I had first met the day before in my shop, had any inkling that today would be the last day she would see her husband alive. I also wondered if I didn't have another investigative story on my hands. Murder is never as clear-cut as it appears and I wondered what the next few days would hold.

Friday, October 4

It was one day before the annual Fall Fest Ball and I was riddled with anxiety. The much-anticipated yacht club dinner and dance had my nerves shot from worrying that some detail had been overlooked. After all, being one of the committee members meant responsibility and this month I had way too much of it.

For now, I needed to concentrate on driving. The early morning sun shimmered off the ocean to my right. Beyond that the waves continued north past Newport, Portsmouth and the infamous Fall River where Lizzie Borden wielded her axe. The story was great fodder for those who loved a good scare, myself included, but somehow this fall season everything seemed more eerie. Maybe my freelance investigative job was getting the best of me.

Whatever the reason, the sheet-ghosts hanging from the trees were spooking me more than normal. I rubbed my neck and patted Cooper on his brown head. I loved my one-hundred-fifteen-pound German shepherd who weighed as much as I did, but then again, I loved all animals. That's why a year ago my husband, Nick, and I had bought a beat-up shingled building in Harbor View, Rhode Island, and I opened my own pet store. Check off one dream fulfilled.

At first glance it would appear we lead a prosaic life. My husband's a dentist who golf's twice a week; we live in a regular-sized fixer-upper in a nice neighborhood; we own a used sailboat and a dog, or should I say the dog owns us; and we feed whatever wildlife scampers, flies or hops into our yard. If it weren't for my part-time freelance investigative writing job, life *would be* mundane. Trouble seems to follow me wherever I go and I wouldn't have it any other way.

The wind was whipping raindrops through the trees and kicking up the fall foliage as I slid the key into the lock of the pet shop. I could hear the phone ringing. Owning a business brings great rewards, but also great demands. Except for Jessica, the part-time college student who helps between classes and poetry readings, I am the sole proprietor of all the stress and anxiety of being a shop owner.

The door-lock was stubborn as I jiggled it to release the catch, but at last it opened. I dropped my purse and work paraphernalia on the wide-pine flooring and grabbed the phone with a breathless, "Hello, Paws for Love. May I help you?"

"I want all of them. Every last one of them for my Mimsey and a few bags of those special homemade treats we always purchase."

I knew for certain what this customer wanted. That strident voice had been grating on my eardrum for almost a year. My hand tightened around the receiver, but I kept my voice calm and cheerful, reminding myself that every demand from Mrs. Wessox translated into the ka-ching of the cash register.

"I can give you four bags of Science Diet Light for...Mimsey, but I need to keep a couple in inventory. I'll be glad to order more today. They should be in by Tuesday."

"If I must wait, but I certainly hope this weather won't escalate into a hideous storm and trap Mimsey and me without her favorite treats. I'll be sending Rutherford over to pick them up later this afternoon." Her tone was accusing.

I didn't see what all of the hullabaloo was about over a little precipitation, but I refrained from voicing my opinion to one of the few remaining matriarchs of Newport society. I had no idea why Mrs. Wessox had chosen my establishment to patronize, but after a year of dealing with her I had come to the conclusion that all the other stores must have politely asked her to take a hike.

"Don't worry, Mrs. Wessox, I promise Mimsey will have plenty of food for the weekend." My tone belied my feelings. I appreciated sincere concern for family pets; I just couldn't stand the upper crust's pretenses.

The conversation ended. Once free of the phone and the desire to pull out my brainstem and jump rope with it on a four-lane highway, I commenced doing what I loved most, playing with the small furry critters I adored so much. My other passion was my freelance job as an investigative reporter.

As I passed by the counter on the way to the storeroom I stopped to finger through the pages of a month-old paper. I kept it around for inspiration. It held what I believed was my best story to date—that of the shocking and horrifying conditions found in puppy mills. Working those few extra hours after the store closed and on weekends was worth the aching back and sleepless nights because my efforts forced those operators to close their doors and never breed dogs again.

I had just finished cleaning the panda-bear hamster cage when the front door swung open, causing the small bell hanging overtop to ring-in a new customer. Stretching over

Cooper and the leftover beef bone he held between his paws, I pushed open the doors separating me from the whitewashed, beadboard counter.

My smile stiffened. Generally I liked all of my customers. I assumed anyone who took care to shop in a premium pet store couldn't be too bad. However, this coiffed individual was a stranger. I prayed this wasn't another Mrs. Wessox; one brainstem is all I have. This chic-looking woman must be someone from Boston, I decided, or maybe even Newport. She appeared able to afford an upscale lifestyle. I assessed her expensive cream linen suit, brown alligator pumps and a wedding ring with a diamond equaling anything owned by Elizabeth Taylor. Slung over her shoulder was a plaid Burberry purse from which peeked the brown-and-white face of a Papillon.

Skipping around the counter I reached out my hand. "Hi, I'm Morgan. May I help you find anything in particular?" I shook the stranger's hand. Her grip was cool and firm, her face serious, her manner formal, but not prudish. At first blush, I liked her.

"Hello. I'm Barbara Voorhees and this is Cocoa," she said, pointing to the small muzzle in her purse. "I don't mean to be discourteous, but Emile, my husband, is waiting for me in the car and we're in a hurry. Could I get a small bag of dog food?" She pointed to a small yellow bag on the lower shelf. "We've been away for the week and I know I'm out at home." She turned her head and her eyes flicked a disdainful look toward the Mercedes parked near the front door.

I saw a man about her age behind the wheel. I surmised marital issues for this woman whose name sounded so familiar, but for now salesmanship was overpowering my recall abilities. "Oh, yes, of course. Is there anything else I can get for you?" I dodged some boxes stacked behind the counter to retrieve the food and a free sample of treats. I placed them on the stainless steel countertop and rang the sale into the register. After an exchange of monies I offered to carry the items to the car, but Mrs. Voorhees scooped up the plastic bag and thanked me for being so efficient before darting out the door.

As the wind howled against the shop's front bay windows, I thought again, *Voorhees, why does that name sound so familiar?* My mind wandered as I watched the darkening clouds pass overhead. I stretched my neck to gaze down the street, past the dock in the distance. The sliver of water I could make out seemed to be churning from underneath, as if by the tumbling of some menacing sea monster, and I struggled wondering why I couldn't shake a feeling of dread.

CHAPTER 2

"Where the heck is Jessica, Cooper? Can she ever be on time for anything in her life? I wonder what excuse it will be today, research paper, or perhaps a poetry reading at the coffee club." I thought out loud shuffling through the week's receipts scattered around my back room desk. "She knew we had to be out of here by two." Cooper looked at me and cocked his large black face to one side as if to say, I feel your anxiety but what do you want me to do about it?

I never let a chance pass by to attribute anthropomorphic qualities to pets, especially Cooper. "I know what you're thinking." I bent down looking him straight in the face. "You're saying, 'if you weren't so easy on her, if you nipped her tardiness in the bud, or let me nip her in the bud once in a while, then maybe she would straighten out her act.'" I stood squaring my shoulders. "Well, when you're right you're right. And today's the day my evil demented twin will let lose its final fury and…"

Just then the back door banged against the wall as a gust of wind hurled in along with my part-time employee. "Hi Mrs. Langdon. Sorry I'm late. Professor Tidby is so long winded." Jessica threw her backpack down, grabbed the broom, and headed straight for the front of the store.

"Hey, wait, I wanted to…talk…to you". But my voice was lost in the banging and scrambling of boxes and bags and cages. "Oh, stop looking at me like that," I growled at Cooper. "At least we might get out of here before she begins a recitation of her newest Gertrude Steinesque brand of poetry. Yuk." But just as I choked out the last word I heard a cacophony of musing coming through the office door.

"What is a fin? A fin so fine. Must I tremble at the sight?" Cooper groaned and I rolled my eyes. "Jessica. Oh, dear Jessica. I'm so glad you're here. We've got to get going or we'll be late for the committee meeting at the yacht club."

"Oh, don't worry about me. I know the routine. Take your time, I'll see you when you get back." She didn't break for a breath, but continued on with her un-metrical lyrics.

I grabbed my purse and dog treats on the way out the door. I was thankful for small favors, like any excuse to be out of the building whenever Jessica decided to share her love of poetry with her furry, feathered and finned wards. One consolation was Jessica loved animals as much as I did and that helped to make her negative attributes less annoying, at least on most days.

Jessica, a sophomore at Salve Regina University, came bounding into *Paws For Love* one Saturday afternoon responding to my help wanted sign I had placed in the window the day before. I didn't know quite what to think of Jessica Lynn Bortelli. She had bleached platinum blond hair, a ring in her eyebrow and a gold stud in her nose. I never could understand the fascination with body piercing. I myself just made it through double ear piercing without falling off the Mall stool, so to make a conscientious decision to inflict more discomfort didn't make sense.

Jessica was tall, at least from my Lilliputian standpoint, with an ebullient demeanor. But it was her rapport with Cooper when I recognized I had a gem of a pet store employee in my midst. Besides, I trusted his instincts. When he pounced out from behind the counter to lay a big wet kiss on her hand I knew she was right for the job. If only Jessica were better with numbers and clocks, which was a constant prayer of mine, then I would have the perfect employee.

Thankfully Harbor View Yacht Club was only a few minutes down the road. I looked at my watch; it was quarter past two. I never did believe in being fashionably late. My car slid to a stop on the gravel driveway, spitting out rocks from my back tires. We both jumped out and rushed up the stamped concrete walk to the double glass doors. The club had spent a fortune last year on the hand etched sailing scenes that graced the entryway, but everyone, including myself, thought it was well worth the expense. I pushed my way in, past the old shelves filled with trophies and paraphernalia from old sailors who had left their mark on Rhode Island's yachting past. I made my apologies to the group seated in the front dining area as we plopped down in our customary places. The room had a cathedral ceiling and dark walnut flooring. Its wide expanse of windows stretched the length of the ballroom and looked over the deep green waters of the north Atlantic. According to all the members this was the room with a view.

The conversation was already in full force as some of the committee members leaned over to give Cooper a welcoming pat on the head. A pint-sized bark greeted them back as he lay down by my feet. These were the times when having passed his Canine Good Citizen test came in handy.

The table was already filled with water glasses and finger foods, compliments of the kitchen staff. Susan Fairfield, who was a doctor of cardiology at Newport General, rested one well-defined arm on the back of her chair. The way she maneuvered the stuffed mushroom into her mouth she appeared more like a seductive movie star than a doctor. She was attractive by anyone's standards. Her sleek chocolate brown hair hung just below her neck and her porcelain flawless thirty something skin said either she could afford the finest facials or genetics were her best friend. While the conversation bubbled she would interject with a snide remark at the most inappropriate times.

To her right was Frank Brower. He was a mousy diminutive man with a speech impediment. He had been living a sheltered life with his wealthy, aging mother for the past forty-four years. Despite his balding head and outdated seventies wire rim glasses, he wasn't unattractive, he just needed a little help from the makeover department. His one biggest asset, besides his millions he would inherit when mommy dearest passed, was his amazing knack for turning a run-of-the-mill party into a night to remember. He was very in touch with his creative side. I had to assume it was because of his stifling domineering parent.

Carol Smith and Diane Handers, both divorcees, had just signed up at the last minute to help with the final details. They had grown-up and lived in Harbor View all their lives and their favorite pastime was to make sure they were invited to every party given within a fifty-mile radius. Everyone appeared to be agreeable until Susan spoke up.

"Can you believe tomorrow night is the annual Fall Fest Ball? How thrilling. It seems like we just finished cleaning up after last years festivities." Her mockery didn't go unnoticed by the others. Susan, who was this year's chairperson, liked having her name on all the committee rosters, but her attitude and actions never seemed to comply with the responsibility that went with the titles.

With a timorous voice that sounded much like Elmer Fudd, Frank Brower spoke up. "*Wealwy* Susan, if you aren't *wilwing* to do the dirty work then you shouldn't be a part of the committee." Frank's battle with his speech demons would get the best of him whenever he was annoyed or nervous; which was a constant whenever Susan was around.

She rolled her eyes showing her disgust for someone whom she considered lily-livered and henpecked. "*Weelwy Fwank*, why don't you worry about your end of the to- do list and I'll worry about mine. Now let's go over this list of RSVP's for dinner requests and see if we've missed anything."

I tried keeping the conversation flowing without having it lapse into an insult free-for-all. "Okay everyone, I'll make notes on all the special request meals. Susan, would you like to do the honors and call off the list?" She shook her head and arranged the papers in front of her. "You three can go over the decoration list and make sure we're not forgetting anything. Does that sound all right with you, Frank," I patted him on the shoulder.

"I'd be *gwad* to." He stood, and with one arm behind his back and the other extended forward he bowed and said, "*Wadies*, shall we go check the centerpieces and make sure they are all up to my usual colorful standards." The girls giggled. Frank looked over his shoulder past Susan's gaze. "We'll be in the room next door if you need anything, Morgan."

Susan was not bothered by the oversight. She couldn't have cared less if Frank gave her the cold shoulder or a cold turkey sandwich.

The RSVP list was quite extensive. The member's roster had grown over the past several years. It was due in part to the renovations the club had made. Also, many Newport folks saw Harbor View Yacht Club as the bourgeois of sailing clubs up until one of its members won last years Bermuda race. Now everyone wanted to be able to rub elbows with the winning team.

I wrote as Susan called off the invitees and their meal requests like a drill sergeant at morning reveille. "Lindenberg-

-two for the Peppered-Crusted Filet Mignon. Hellman--three for the Trout Almandine. Voorhees--one trout and a special note for one filet mignon, no salt. Yes, absolutely no salt," Susan interjected with a snide smile. "Fredericks. One…." Susan's voiced trailed off into the distance as my mind began wandering back to my early morning customer.

"Voorhees. Is that why that name rang a bell?" I pulled the meal ticket out from under Susan's hand.

"Hey, we're way past Voorhees. Come on. Keep up Morgan. I've got to get back to the hospital by five." She grabbed it back and placed it in the done pile.

"Sorry. It's just I met Mrs. Voorhees this morning in my store and I knew the name sounded familiar. I must have seen it before when we were sending out the invitations. She appeared…moneyed." I paused to think of a tactful description. "She and her husband stopped by to pick up some dog food for...um…Cocoa. Yeah, that's it." I was always better at remembering dog's names than people.

"Isn't that quaint? I don't know why you'd think she's so special. What's the big deal about one more well to-do family with a Mercedes? There are a million of them around here. In fact I'm one of them. Now let's get back to business." She chortled to herself as if she had some hidden agenda then continued down the list forcing me to think of nothing but writing at warp speed.

It was an hour later and the group was finishing the final details when Art Leadbetter, the head chef made his way out from the kitchen. He was average build, but had a better than average middle-aged look with his graying temples and dark brooding eyes. His most noticeable trait, though, was his luxuriant full head of salt and pepper hair. The kind women love to run their hands through. He had come to live in Harbor View less then six months ago after retiring from his own restaurant in Boston. The death of his wife and daughter in a car accident and the fast paced life of restaurant ownership had become too much. I worried the Yacht clubs schedule may be more than he had bargained for.

"Hi Art." Not following any of Emily Posts rules, I stuffed a few bites of leftovers into my mouth. With a compliment of flavors rolling around my tongue I had to tuck in some escaping crumbs before I could manage a, "Thanks so much for the watercress sandwiches, and this cracker-spread stuff. It's so yummy."

Art, who came across avuncular where I was concerned, chuckled at my lack of culinary wordage and possibly my unladylike behavior. He did appreciate the flattery just the same. "How's every thing else going?"

"We've got our list compiled and organized for you. As usual, there are a few specialty orders." I fingered through the list. "Mrs. Wessox wants extra Boursin cheese in her chicken and Mr. Flinch doesn't want any almonds on his trout almandine". I shook my head at the nonsense of certain members.

Art acquiesced with a shake of his shoulders. "Don't worry. I could tell you stories about some of my customers in Boston that would curl your toes. What else is there?"

"Well, our newest member, Mr. Emile Voorhees, seems to have the only legitimate request. No salt on his steak. Hope this won't be too much of a hassle for you." I waited for a response. "Earth to Art," I said touching his arm.

He looked down and smiled, "Oh, I'm sorry. I was off thinking about another private party I'm throwing this weekend. It seems like there's been one right after another this past month. I suppose with the holidays approaching it's not going to slow down in the near future. Don't worry about it, that's my job. I'll be back here tomorrow afternoon if you have any last minute requirements." With that said, he untied his apron and waved as he left the room.

I walked past the large folding doors that separated the two dining areas. To my left were a few of the 6-foot round tables with all the centerpieces. They were replicas of antique oil lamps. Curled around the bases were the orange and red-berried branches of bittersweet vine. They were simplistic but perfect, because even though bittersweet is considered an invasive plant, it symbolizes fall to me. Much of the bittersweet actually grew on the property of the club so it had been convenient to use for this event. Holding it all together was a fine organza ribbon that flowed in and around the berries. The night of the Ball we would pull names to win a centerpiece. All in all I was quite proud of the work we had done and told everyone so, but I knew most of the creativeness came from Frank. So as to not let a good thought go unspoken, I leaned over and whispered, "This wouldn't have come together so beautifully if it weren't for you. Thanks." Frank lowered his shining scalp and smiled.

"Tomorrow we will have to *stwing* the little white lights. The trees won't arrive from the nursery until two, so let's arrive right before then if that's okay with everyone?" He saw affirmative nods from Diane and me. He got an encouraging squeeze on the shoulder from Carol. With that Frank picked up his canvas bag and didn't wait for a smart aleck rebuttal from Susan and headed for the front door. Poor Frank, I thought. Just a little encouragement helped to calm his speech nerves. I hoped the night of the ball he would be in good form. I promised myself I would compliment his artistic prowess as much as I could. Hopefully his insecurities would be buoyed enough to make it through the evening. I hated to see what Susan might have in store for him if he greeted people sounding like Elmer Fudd. He was such a sweet guy.

Even divorced Carol seemed to think he had potential. According to her he had dreamboat eyes and a sexy butt. I didn't see it, but what did it matter, Carol did, that's all that counted. They were two peas from the same pod as far as I was concerned. Despite Nick's desperate attempts to discourage me from playing matchmaker, I had a plan to push the two of them together and the Fall Fest Ball would be just the place, come nor'easter or shine.

CHAPTER 3

Gusts of wind were buzzing like bees around a hive by the time I got back to work. I checked in on Jessica to make sure the numbers balanced at the end of the day and then locked up for the evening. Jessica wasn't a genius with numbers, but she could always work on Saturdays. That was a benefit because it gave Cooper and me time to volunteer wherever we were needed. Usually that meant nursing homes, but once in a while we visited kids at the local hospital. Tomorrow, however, I would stray from the norm and help prepare for the Fall Fest Ball.

I arrived home just in time to greet my husband as he came through the back door. Our house was much like all the other cedar-shingled homes on the coast of Rhode Island, but it offered a glimmer of old English cottage with its stone facade and climbing ivy. "Hi, honey. How was your day?" I asked.

He gave me a peck on the forehead. "The wind sure is pounding up the waves. We'll need to keep checking the satellite pictures on the Internet. Maybe the committee will have to cancel the shindig tomorrow night." This was Nick's way of saying he hoped for a reprieve from an all-night tuxedo, but I ignored him by opening and closing kitchen cabinets in search of dinner.

"There's nothing to eat." Discouraged, I plopped into a ladder-back chair, flung my feet onto the cushioned window seat and exclaimed, "It's Chinese from Wong Fu's tonight. How's that sound?"

Knowing he wasn't getting a choice of restaurants, Nick said, "Chinese sounds great." We were out the door and filling ourselves with fried rice and sweet-and-sour chicken in a matter of minutes. Much to Cooper's chagrin, he wasn't invited to go along.

Saturday, October 5

It was the day of the ball and Nick shuffled into the kitchen, his chewed-up suede slippers barely clinging to his feet. "You're sure you're going to be back in time to help me with my penguin suit, right?" he asked with a pained look on his face. Ignoring him, I finished pouring a cup of steaming hazelnut coffee into my travel mug. Cooper was sitting by the back door with his leash dangling from his mouth.

"Please stop grumbling. I need to be at the club for a couple of hours to help set up. Then I'll be home. You'd think I was asking you to get a root canal the way you're fussing about tonight." Out of the corner of my eye I caught an annoyed look. Being a dentist, he didn't find dental analogies very amusing.

Reaching on tiptoes, I kissed his stubbly face, patted the dog and whisked myself out the door. "And don't forget to take Cooper for a walk," I called back over my shoulder.

Besides the kitchen staff and the tree rental company, I was the first to arrive at the club. I took on the job of moving the round tables into position on the dance floor as the other committee members began filtering in. They entered one by one, first Frank then Carol and Diane. They were all shaking off the first signs of a heavy drizzle, and made their way past the miniature Japanese maples clustered together near the corner of the room.

Frank Broward laid his trench coat on the nearest chair, scanned the room and asked with disdain, "Isn't Susan *hewe* yet?" Frank's speech impediment was pronounced but I was used to it. So was everyone else. I liked the man tremendously and didn't mind one bit if he occasionally struggled with his *r*'s and his *l*'s.

Frank's usual quiet resolve was melting into impatience. "After all, she is the committee *chaiwman*. You'd think she would have been the first to arrive. Instead, like always, everyone else *compwetes* half the *wowk*, and then she waltzes in and takes all the *cwedit.*"

"Not that I'm defending her, but she is a doctor. It's possible she had an emergency at the hospital," I said.

"More than likely her *emewgency* was getting her nails done. I *sweaw* that woman should have gone into plastic *suwgery* as her specialty with the amount of time she spends on herself."

Carol Smith rolled her eyes as she blew on her nails and then polished them on her shoulder. Frank looked down at the floor trying to suppress a laugh. This was one more sign that screamed Carol and Frank should go on a date. My dilemma was that Frank would be the last person to make the first move and Carol was from the old school of wait-for-the-man-to do-the-asking. It was obvious they needed some encouragement to get things moving. I began whistling a tune from *Fiddler on the Roof* with great enthusiasm.

As we were about to give up on our intrepid leader, Susan strolled in looking svelte in a handsome rust-colored suede skirt and silk blouse. Her outfit was quite a contrast to the blue jeans, T-shirts and oxfords everyone else was wearing.

"Don't you look pretty, Susan," Carol said, looking down at her own untucked bright-red T-shirt that read, *I rode the Matterhorn-1996*.

"Yes, you look very *shawp*, but that's not the outfit you should be *weawing* for what we have to do. Did you *bwing* a change of clothes?" Frank asked.

Mystified at Susan's obliviousness, I shook my head and continued moving tables while Frank and some of the other committee members slid the trees into place around the dance floor.

In defense of herself, Susan said, "You must have forgotten, but we still need name cards for the tables. I thought I could use the computer in the office to enter the RSVP's and print them off. I brought everything I'll need. If anyone's looking for me I'll be down the hall." She didn't wait for a response but turned, disappearing down the hall in her four-inch suede heels.

I had to admit I'd forgotten about the name cards, but Susan's manner did little to console the group. We knew the rest of us would be stuck with all the schlepping.

At exactly four thirty-two I stole a glance at the large nautical clock hanging high in the eave of the ballroom. "Holy mackerel. We've all got to get home, get changed and get back here by six. Cocktails start at six fifteen" A slight panic attack rose in my voice.

Susan had left an hour earlier, leaving the pile of name cards with their table numbers in a basket by the front entrance. We scrambled to place them, conceding that the "room with a view" had never looked better. Now the only thing needed was a miracle that the storm would hold off for everyone to arrive safe and dry.

"See you at six." I waved to everyone, grabbing an old umbrella that had long been forgotten in the coat stand and running through the puddles left behind from an all-day drizzle.

Nick was home in the bedroom pacing, half-dressed waiting for direction. Cooper followed him like a good soldier. I stood staring at them from the doorway, shaking my head in amazement. How could someone so intelligent be so unfocused and disorganized when out of his element? Fifty minutes later, after letting out the dog, showering and throwing in a load of laundry, I was tying Nick's bowtie and putting on my lipstick. I could multitask with the best of them.

The officers of the yacht club arrived early, turned on the tree lights and lit the oil lamps. By the time Nick and I arrived, I felt I was walking into a Grace Kelly movie, me in my black strapless Vera Wang knockoff and Nick in a classic Cary Grant tuxedo. The only unattractive item in the picture was the large bright-green golf umbrella we were forced to carry as a shield from what was becoming a torrential downpour. Still, the yacht club glowed from within with what looked like hundreds of tiny fireflies swarming in unison to the beat of Bobby Darin crooning *Beyond the Sea.*

Abandoning the awkward umbrella in the hall and stepping inside the ballroom, Nick admired the layout. "It looks beautiful. You did a great job, honey. Everyone will have a wonderful time thanks to you and the committee." Nick squeezed my shoulder with pride and grabbed our assigned seating from the registration table. "Now where are those hors d'oeuvres you keep raving about and do you think the bar TV is open? They're showing recaps of the golf tournament on ESPN tonight." In a wink he was off. I sighed realizing some things—such as husbands with one-track minds—never change.

The commodore and his wife, Mr. and Mrs. Lyle Livingston, were the official greeters for the evening. Mrs. Livingston was the quintessential yacht club wife. With every event she managed to pull off the nautical look in a classic style. This night was no exception. She complemented her husband's old naval uniform with her dark-blue satin gown embroidered with gold stars around the bodice. The pair made a handsome couple.

I joined the other committee members standing shoulder-to-shoulder behind the registration table. We handed out seating assignments and raffle tickets to win, at evening's end, the wreaths and lamps that served as centerpieces on the tables. Even Susan had managed to arrive on time, standing in place at the edge of the table nearest the door.

The guests began filtering in at a snail's pace. I feared the storm would make people reluctant to attend, but gradually the room filled with the sounds of boating conversations, clinking glasses and laughter.

"Hello, Mr. And Mrs. Handrahan. I saw slip number five opened up for you." He shook his head and gave half a smile. I continued making cordial conversation, my fingers filing through the H's. "Here's where you'll be seated, and here's a raffle ticket. Good luck and enjoy the evening." I was affable as I could be, but I sensed here was another male partygoer who didn't relish the formal attire.

"Mr. Flinch, nice to see you this evening." Susan handed him his table tag. It bore a notation written in red by the kitchen staff: NA, which meant no almonds.

Susan leaned into my shoulder after he passed by. "He's as crazy as a loon. What normal person would order trout almandine without the almonds? That's like saying, 'Give me a rum and Coke without the rum.'"

I wasn't sure about the analogy, but I had to agree. Thankfully there were only a few specialty orders that head chef Art and his kitchen staff would have to deal with this evening.

The cracking thunder created an atmosphere more like Halloween than a harvest ball as the final members arrived at the club. Emile and Barbara Voorhees were among the last that chose to brave the weather in tux and gown. Emile made his way past the rest of the committee to the end of the table and announced himself to Frank. There were very few last names beginning with *V*, so it didn't take Frank long to locate Voorhees. "Here you go, sir. Good *wuck* on the *waffel*." Frank said.

Voorhees grabbed the tags and ticket, placed an arm around his wife's waist and marched her to their table.

"Nice going, *Fwank*. Have you ever thought of getting speech therapy? There's nothing worse then paying a hundred and fifty dollars to attend a function and then walking into a Looney Tunes cartoon instead," Susan railed. She grabbed her purse and stomped off to order a drink.

Carol began muttering reassurances to soothe Frank's hurt feelings. I chose this opportune moment to leave the two of them alone and go search for my husband. I was certain he was still immersed in the tournament's leader board at the bar TV. I caught him scrutinizing some professional golfer's swing. I tapped him on the shoulder. "Don't you think we should go find where we're sitting? I think Frank placed us at a table over there." I pointed to the one nearest the hall leading to the bathrooms.

"That's the best the committee members can get?" Nick said, probably disheartened by the prospect of bathroom fumes wafting past his nostrils.

"I know it's not the greatest seating, but we wanted to leave the best tables for the VIPs."

"That would be the Very Insipid Party-poopers?" he replied.

"Thinking on our feet, are we? Cheer up, Nick. Lack of substance and wealth don't always go hand in hand." But my timing was off. Just then Frank's mother hurled herself through the front door. By sheer good fortune Frank was there to open it; if he hadn't, she would surely have shattered a few thousand dollars worth of etched glass.

Raising one eyebrow, Frank's mother, Amanda Broward, announced in a supercilious tone that *the man* was parking her car. She threw off her rain jacket allowing it to drop on the registration table. My first impression was that she looked like a character from a 1960s *Twilight Zone* episode. Her dress was an Audrey Hepburn'ish long-sleeve crepe with an asymmetrical neckline. It looked haute couture but it smelled like mothballs. The fabric clung to a body thirty pounds heavier than the garment was designed to fit and the rest of her wasn't much better. She'd had so much cosmetic work done, her face looked like a fruit bowl stretched with plastic wrap. Her lips showed signs of collagen injections. They were plumper than was natural, but they seemed to fit her darkly lined, drooping eyes. I could smell vermouth on her breath when she passed by me a few feet away.

Waving a rain dripping hand like Queen Elizabeth, she demanded at the top of her voice, "Frank, show me to my table. I can't believe you and your committee members found it appropriate to host a gala on such a hideous evening." Without a word, the dutiful son escorted her to the table at the farthest end of the room. I suspected this arrangement wasn't accidental.

"Okay, so I'm not always right." I gave Nick a smirk and grabbed him by the cuff, ushering him to our table.

Nick sat reluctantly while I remembered one more committee contribution I promised to make. I went to find the club's digital camera to get shots for next month's newsletter. On my way toward the back office, I passed the Voorhees's table.

"I hope you remembered my pills. You know I'm supposed to take them with food," Emile Voorhees said. He jerked his wife's purse off a chair and onto the table.

"Yes, dear, I've got them." Barbara Voorhees rummaged through her Louis Vuitton bag and extracted a small green bottle. With shaking hands she snapped it open, giving a capsule to Emile who popped it down with a swig of water while waiting for dinner to be served.

The evening progressed trouble-free. The waiters looked perfect with their appetizer trays held high above their tuxedoed shoulders. The acoustic system made the recorded sounds of Billie Holiday and Frank Sinatra sound live, twenty feet away. I could imagine Benny Goodman raising his baton to conduct a forty-man orchestra. Feet tapped and dancers whirled through the four-course meal. Art Leadbetter, with his tall white chef's cap, went from table to table, making sure everything was to the members' liking. The special dinner requests went off without a hitch. I ran around getting photos of it all in both color and black-and-white, occasionally stopping by my plate for a quick bite of food. I finally landed as dessert was being served

Nick leaned over, hand outstretched. "Do you want to take a spin around the dance floor?"

"Honey, I've been around the dance floor ten times." I lifted the camera. "Besides, I want to eat my tiramisu. It's the only real dinner I'm going to get. Try me again in about thirty minutes." I shooed him away and suggested he ask Diane Sanders, who had come without an escort. Nick gave me his sad puppy-dog look; which was meant to elicit guilt, but I was too exhausted and hungry to care. With a bit of coaxing he left, blowing me a kiss halfway across the dance floor.

I leaned back and stretched my arms in hopes of reenergizing myself. I considered jogging around the table a dozen times, but decided a few more teaspoons of sugar in my coffee could accomplish the same thing. The music played on as I sat watching Nick and Diane twirl around the dance floor and sipped the last remnant of my second cup of coffee. It wasn't quite as good as the stuff at Café Java on Main Street, but considering they were making it a gallon at a time, it wasn't bad. My relaxing interlude was interrupted when I turned to see Emile Voorhees walking toward the back hall, just yards away from my table. Silhouetted against the blue wall, with a long leg outstretched from the slit of her gold dress, was Susan. A seductive look shone in her eyes. I couldn't help but think her silken figure gave the appearance of an alluring spider spinning a web, contemplating her prey. Her come-hither glance projected itself across the room straight toward Emile Voorhees. The pheromones encircling the two of them were palpable, even at this distance.

I didn't remember Susan mentioning she knew Voorhees, and my curiosity reared its ugly head. I slid my wooden chair a few feet in their direction. This spontaneous movement caused my chair to make a scratching sound across the floor and I feared I would be detected. I felt a rosy blush rising in my cheeks. The possibility of embarrassment didn't, however, stop me from tuning my listening up a notch.

Voorhees's urgent request to Susan was muffled. I leaned back farther, almost falling over before catching myself by my fingertips under the edge of the table. That move was unnecessary. The next words out of Susan's mouth could be heard above the din, if anyone were interested in listening, which I was.

"You told me you were coming alone this evening or is this just one more of your many lies?"

Emile grabbed her arm, pulling her away from the wall and into his chest. "Keep your voice down. I can come with whomever I want and tonight it's my wife. Besides, you need to start letting go. It's over. I'm not about to lose a few million over some silly affair." He released his grip, leaving Susan obviously crushed by his remark. For once she had been silenced, but the reprieve was only momentary. They say hell hath no fury like a woman scorned; now I knew exactly what that adage meant.

At first her face held no emotion. "You made me think I was the only one. That I was going to be the last affair you ever had. How could I have been such a fool? It was just a ploy for cheap sex." Her face transformed from stoic to flaming red. "You'll never be able to keep your brain zipped up, will you, Emile? Eventually Barbara's going to wise up. I guess I have nothing to lose by letting her in on our little secret. You hurt me, Emile, and I'll hurt you. An eye for an eye, don't you think?" Susan's eyes glowed like molten steel.

He squeezed her against him, tighter than before, and issued a warning. "I can cause just as much damage, sweetheart, or have you forgotten who's on our conservative hospital board?"

Susan's fury rose. She turned, strode in my direction, then stopped a few feet away and called back over her smooth, rounded shoulder, "You'll pay for your indiscretions and I'll be the one collecting." Her dark brown chignon broke loose spilling her silky hair across her back. "And it may be sooner than you bargained for," she added, marching away in cadence to the resonating bass drum.

Emile pulled a handkerchief from his front pocket and wiped the sweat from his forehead. Then as if his tryst had been nothing more than a walk on the beach, he returned to his faithful wife.

Nick was always complaining that nothing interesting ever happened at these soirees; well did I have a revelation for him. Just as I resolved to drag my husband away from whatever distraction was gripping him at the moment, he showed up, smiling. He looked at me with dark hazel eyes and a loving, but quizzical, expression. He knew my facial countenances all too well, for the first words out of his mouth were, “What have you been up to? You have that look you get when you’re on a writing assignment.”

In a whisper I recounted to Nick what I’d seen and heard—and the lengths I had gone to eavesdrop.

Nick shook his head in disbelief. “It’s moments like this that make me worry about your sanity,” He said. “Let me ask you something. Have you ever been bitten by a fruit bat? That’s the only explanation for those big ears of yours.” He gestured with his hands splayed out beside his head. “Oh, never mind.” He grabbed my hand and pulled me out of my chair. “You need a spin around the dance floor. I can tell you put way too much sugar in your coffee again.”

Nick held me close around my waist as we glided by the handful of singles who braved the night without a date.

“Look at Carol and Frank standing on opposite sides of the floor, each wishing the other would ask for a dance,” I whispered in Nick’s ear. “Don’t you think those two would make a cute couple? They have so much in common.”

“Morgan, when will you ever learn? If they are meant to get together, they will. They don’t need a push from you.” Exasperation was in his voice. I seldom heard that tone from Nick.

I loosened my husband’s grip and took over the lead, coasting us to a stop by Frank and his stalwart mother who were standing by their table. “Are you two having a nice time this evening?”

Amanda Broward, who was never short on condescending comments, said in her most blue-blooded enunciation, "If you must have my opinion…" She paused formulating her response. "I am disappointed the chef couldn't have chosen a more elegant menu. What was he thinking? Basic steak and trout dishes, really! What about coalfish with farigoule, or scallops and champagne?" I was almost impressed until Mrs. Broward hiccupped into her martini and swayed back into her chair missing the floor by mere inches.

Sensing Mrs. Broward was enjoying her drink far more than her son's company, I took him aside. I pride myself on being honest to a fault, but sometimes I feel the need to wander over to the deviant side to get things accomplished. With that in mind, and ignoring Nick's get-back-over-here look, I murmured into Frank's ear, "Carol didn't want to bother you and your mother, but she was wondering, whenever you could squeeze in a moment, if you would like to dance?" I anticipated his answer.

"She *weawy* wants to dance with me? Well, I'm sure Mother wouldn't mind, would you, Mother?" His mother was busy harassing the waiter so I choose to drag him half way across the floor letting him go off on his own like a fledgling leaving the nest.

I returned to Nick grinning like the Cheshire cat and followed his lead spinning past the expansive windows. Large raindrops pummeled the panes. No one seemed to notice or care that a fierce storm was descending upon Harbor View. Maybe it was the music and the full stomachs. More than likely it was the massive quantities of alcohol being passed over the bar every few minutes. Thankfully, the committee members were wise enough to keep the inhabitants of the community safe from blurry vision and less-than-sharp instincts. We had hired a limousine service to transport the inebriated home in one piece.

"I'm worried about Cooper," I said, "I hope he's not nervous from the storm. Maybe we should go home and check on him?"

"Honey, I'm sure he's lying in front of the TV watching *Animal Planet.* Besides, you got me into this penguin outfit, so you might as well enjoy it for a while." He paused. "Anyway, we'll be home in an hour or so. He'll be fine." Nick pulled me closer, making me feel as if everything were right with the world.

The lights flickered as thunder clapped outside. We paused to take a breather by the opened doorway, and enjoy a glass of Reisling we had snagged when gliding by the bar. We peered out the last set of French doors leading onto a large covered cedar deck. Sweaty partygoers, I imagined, must have opened the doorway to catch a cool, if not a bit misty, evening breeze. Beyond the deck grew beach bramble; past that stretched a glistening expanse of sand that sloped into the now fierce sea. Because of the foreboding weather and the large puddles being created from the storm, I was surprised to hear voices coming from outside.

"I think, Voorhees, you have forgotten who you're dealing with. My business may be legitimate now, but it doesn't mean I don't have ties to the Old World."

"Is that a threat, Taglianno? If you're so almighty respectable then take me to court. If not, we've got nothing more to say to each other."

I stole a quick glance at Nick as I moved behind the small portion of wall separating each set of six windows. These solid spaces stretched around the circumference of the ballroom. I wasn't an engineer, but I believed they were for hanging artwork, not supporting the ceiling. I motioned with my index finger for Nick to follow. He acquiesced with a begrudging grin.

In a low voice, he said, "What do you think you're doing? Can't you see that's a private conversation? I sometimes think you should work for the *National Enquirer.* Your curiosity…well, you know what they say about the cat."

I shushed him with a finger to my lip. "Don't you know who that is?" I whispered. "That's Tony Taglianno of the infamous Tag-li-an-no family from Boston."

A glimmer of recognition passed across Nick's face.

"That's right, you do remember," I said. "How can you not be interested?"

"Because cement shoes and missing fingers are not anything I find appealing. Now come on. We're leaving before they catch us eavesdropping."

Just then the discussion outside crescendoed into an argument heated enough to freeze Nick in his shiny black oxfords and me in my high-heeled satin pumps.

Taglianno's voice rose to a feverish pitch. He thrust a finger into Voorhees's chest, causing him to lose his balance. "I may do just that and more. We've had this conversation one too many times. This is going to be the last. How about I let your partner know what you've been up to? I'm sure he'd be interested in how you've been extorting extra profit on the side."

Taking two steps forward to invade Taglianno's personal space, Voorhees leaned in almost nose-to-nose and said, "You can't prove anything, so get out of my face."

Taglianno moved away, straightened his jacket and uttered with the calmness of a spring breeze, "I'll get my restitution, one way or the other. Then you can talk to me about proof when you're walking the path to perdition." He nodded his dismissal and headed through the French doors not seeming to notice our backs turned away from the cool night air and any suspicious looks.

I peered back over my shoulder at the man left outside. Voorhees's cavalier demeanor withered as he grabbed for a plastic outdoor chair. He collapsed into it as if in a slow motion movie scene. The wind drove a sheet of rain onto the covered deck, spraying Voorhees who didn't seem to notice or care.

Nick's facial expression shifted from cautious curiosity to tangible fear. "Let's go home, honey. I've had enough of stiff ties and death threats for one night."

"Oh, come on. The evening's just getting interesting. Let's stay another hour. It will only be nine thirty. Ple-e-ease."

"So much for worrying about the pooch," he said, as he succumbed to my plea. He often says living with me is like being lost at sea in a raging storm, but on a really nice yacht. You have all the amenities you can ask for, but the ride sure can get bumpy.

As predicted, the real storm was turning nastier by the minute. A cold front was moving in fast and the sky held no starlight. The frenetic rhythm of the rain and wind caused several of the partygoers to hang up their dancing shoes early in the evening and leave before eight thirty. However, those who tried to leave after nine were forced to return to the club. The only exit road ran across a small inlet bridge, which was now flooded over.

The club's commodore, Lyle Livingston, announced over the microphone that no one could leave for a while, but that desserts and coffee would be available as long as needed. The DJ returned to his job, popping CDs into his system and turning up the volume. By now many members were seated sipping hot drinks laced with alcohol in hopes of quelling their storm-sequestered anxieties.

The Voorheeses were one of the few couples still left on the dance floor. Showing genuine concern for her husband,

Barbara Voorhees said, “Emile, you don’t look well. Maybe we should sit down.”

“Stop babying me, Barbara. You were the one who wanted to come so we could dance, so let’s dance.” He grabbed her around the waist as if he needed to steady himself, not sway to the beat of a jazz song. Sweat beads trickled down his flushed face as he turned toward the bar, at first staring indiscriminately, then transfixed on something in the distance.

“Maybe you’re right,” he said. “I need to rest my head from the music. I’m going back to one of the offices and sit for a while. Don’t bother me. I’ll come out when I’m ready.” He left her on the floor staring at him as he walked away, head down, shoulders hunched.

Being a stalwart people observer, I noticed their every move. He left, leaving Barbara looking hurt. She gazed about as if hoping no one noticed her husband’s callous demeanor. I felt sorry for her. She seemed lost in a sea of unfamiliar faces. I watched as she shuffled back to her table and sat in silence.

The lights flickered as we jitterbugged and line danced our way through the late evening, trying to ignore the apparent storm surge. The loud music did nothing to conceal the crashing thunder, which was becoming more intense as the storm passed overhead. An unearthly feeling tingled down my back as the thunder rolled and a scream vibrated the air. Then as though someone had pulled a switch, everything went quiet and dark.

CHAPTER 4

Barbara Voorhees came stumbling down the hall, crying that she'd found her husband, dead. She was right, I realized, as I followed Susan Fairchild into Art Leadbetter's office.

Emile Voorhees lay on a small leather couch. A knife protruded from his back.

Susan set her lamp on a small table near the body. Shifting shadows danced around the room. "This was murder," she said softly. "Did anyone reach 9-1-1?"

"The cell-phone signals aren't getting through." Nick, who had followed the light of the oil lamp, whispered behind me, "No one seems to be able to get through on the landline, either. The wires must be down."

Susan's face took on a ghoulish appearance as she raised the lamp closer to get a better look. It wouldn't matter if the emergency medical services arrived within a few seconds. Death's dark shadow was already circulating through the room.

We stood silent for a moment until I snapped out of my frozen state and mustered a calm, official tone. "We'd better not touch anything. We don't want to disturb any trace or latent evidence."

Nick lifted an eyebrow. He appeared impressed with my quick analysis and calm handling of the situation, but in truth, I simply watch too much television. We left the door, as it was, halfway open. Nick and I each put an arm around Barbara's waist and walked her back to her table. I pushed the plates back from the edge, sat her down and handed her a glass of water. Picking up the black silk scarf lying across Emile's chair, I placed it over her sagging shoulders. "We should keep quiet for now about your husband." I whispered.

She didn't respond.

The room glowed in the lantern light, and wall shadows shifted as the club members waited to hear what had happened. Not wanting to create hysteria by using the word *murder*, I made an instantaneous decision to mask the truth. "It appears Emile Voorhees has died," I said. "I'm certain once the emergency services get here, they'll be able to tell us more."

A unified sigh of sadness reverberated and chairs scraped the floor as some of the partygoers sat back down and others moved across the room to comfort Barbara.

As if on cue, Art brushed by me with a basketful of candles. He called out to everyone. "These should help keep you going until the storm lets up," he promised. "The stainless steel pots will keep the coffee hot for an hour or so. Everyone just help yourselves."

The partygoers seemed relieved. The instant gratification of hot coffee, for the time being, was more alluring than the possibility of rescue from the storm. Art handed out candles and logo matchbooks one by one. He made the mistake of offering the items to Amanda Broward.

"Don't hand that to me. The only time I want melting wax near my skin is at the spa!" She jerked away from him and crossed her legs.

"I'll take that last one," Frank said politely, lighting it as he walked toward me. His brow was scrunched with concern. "What happened exactly?" he asked. "I mean, was it an accident or a heart attack? Your face is telling more than you're saying," he mumbled into my ear.

"You're a pretty perceptive guy," I said. "Listen, this is on the q. t." I knew he could keep a secret because I knew how often he needed to skirt his mother's nosiness. I took him aside, leaned head-to-head and whispered what truth I knew.

Frank's jaw dropped.

"We need to keep this quiet for now," I cautioned. "In the meantime, I noticed Carol sitting alone at her table. Why don't you go over and keep her company?"

"Well, I *weawwy* should get back to Mother."

"Frank, your mom's enjoying nagging the help with her one-of-a-kind pretentious behavior, and I mean that in the kindliest way. Now go."

I noticed Susan was checking her watch, possibly making a note of the time for the coroner. Then she walked over to the bar and quickly tossed back someone's half-full cocktail. I watched Susan and checked my watch at the same time: ten twenty-two. I chalked this up to reporter's obsession with details. It started in my college days when I learned to get the facts straight on the five basic W's of journalism: who, what, when, where, and why.

I then went in search of Nick, who had decided to guard the hallway against curiosity seekers. Before I reached him, Art tapped my shoulder. "Is there anything else I can do to help?" he asked.

"Thanks, no. Except you'd better stay out of your office." Art's bewildered expression forced me to think on my toes. If the truth were to be told, it wouldn't come from me, at least not until law enforcement arrived and gave the okay. "Emile died in your office, and in cases like this I'm sure that protocol demands leaving the scene undisturbed until the police say otherwise." I hoped he would accept this as fact.

"Oh, sure, no problem. There's nothing in there I can't live without, for a while anyway." He set off for the kitchen, oil lamp in hand.

Some subconscious notion was angling its way through my brain. I was prone to a hyperactive imagination, but this feeling was more than an overreaction. I knew Nick would nip my curiosity in the derrière if he knew I was looking for an angle. I decided to keep quiet for the time being, recognizing full well that even a brief period of silence would be a miraculous accomplishment for me.

Rain and wind still pelted the exterior of the club, and rescue from the darkness was still not in sight when Frank stood on the stage and notified the group that he had gotten through to 9-1-1. The rescue services were not certain when they could arrive. If the road was still too flooded, the emergency dispatcher said she would try sending the Coast Guard helicopter to remove the body, but there was no guarantee of how long everyone else would have to stay. Moans of frustration floated through the room and stopped at me.

I was encouraged by the delay. It wasn't that I wanted to corrupt the evidence. I simply wanted a chance to get the scoop before any other reporters and the police got involved. This could be quite an article. I could see the spin already: a night of merriment, the murder of a prominent citizen and the reactions of the influential partygoers who were privy to the night's events. *What a coup!* Just as I was dreaming of an award-winning story, Nick nudged me back to reality with a warm hand on my neck.

"Where were you? You looked a million miles away." Without mentioning all my motivations, I admitted I was contemplating a story for *The Journal.*

"This is *murder*, not some poor devil who got robbed of his baseball card collection," Nick said. "In fact, the murderer could be one of us." He cast a suspicious glance around the room.

Feeling miffed that he hadn't remembered my more gutsy articles; I did my best to ignore his slight. "Exactly," I said. "I need to get the facts while they're still hot. Besides, it could have been an outsider who made his way through the back door. The murderer is probably long gone by now." My eyes twinkled.

"Oh, right, and he would have gone where? Over the flooded inlet in a dinghy he had waiting for him? I'm going to be keeping my eye on you. There could be a psycho running loose." He crossed his arms and glared at me the way a father eyes a precocious child.

"I'll be careful. Besides, I'm receiving that tingle down my spine that I get when something doesn't seem quite right."

"Honey, you get that same feeling when my mother comes to visit, so what is that supposed to mean?"

I gave him my, you're-impossible look, and wandered off to find Susan Fairfield. Motives for murder were lingering in the air and Susan would be a good place to start. Her earlier conversation with Voorhees didn't bode well for her perfect doctor image. I found her a few moments later standing by an open doorway. She was nursing another drink as she looked up at me, eyes glistening. "You know, I always thought it would be his heart that gave out on him, but I'm not surprised it ended this way."

Dumbfounded, I wondered if she was responding to her clinical intuition or guilt. "Why would you say that? Do you know something that could help the police?"

Susan looked away and turned to catch a breeze that lifted her hair off her creamy shoulders. "Now that he's dead, I suppose there's no more patient confidentiality." She paused to collect her thoughts. "He came in for a few appointments because of angina attacks. The tests showed he had high blood pressure and high cholesterol. He looked great on the outside, but his insides were crap. I put him on medication, but he thought he was invincible. Not that any of that matters now.

He obviously didn't die from something he ate, now did he?" Her sneer didn't go unnoticed.

I ignored it and said, "He must have been concerned about his diet. Remember, he did ask for no salt on his meal."

"Oh." Susan looked away into the darkness. "Well, his wife must have harped on him to watch his diet and take his pills. What does it matter now anyway?" She chugged back the last swallow from her glass tumbler. "I need another one. If you'll excuse me."

Susan was turning to walk away when I reached out a finger and tapped her on the shoulder. "Just one more thing. You weren't shocked he was murdered. Is there something else I should know, say for instance the conversation I overheard between you and Emile earlier this evening? I didn't mean to eavesdrop; it's just that your tête-à-tête was a bit resounding."

"Who do you think you are, some kind of female Columbo? You look more like Nancy Drew to me." She eyed me up and down. "The conversation may have been loud, but it was still private, and that's the way it's going to stay." She turned with shoulders squared and stomped off toward the bar.

She sure can handle her alcohol, I thought. I assumed her over-consumption was reserved for special occasions. Hoping the next encounter wouldn't be as confrontational I contemplated how I should approach Taglianno. I didn't relish the idea of angering someone who only a few years earlier had given up his Mafia ties. At least that was the impression leftover from the local papers and floating rumors. I strolled around the room and found the Tagliannos sitting arm-in-arm at a vacant table. I approached with the leeriness of a chipmunk ascending from his hole.

"Hello, Mr. and Mrs. Taglianno. I'm Morgan Langdon. I'm on the Fall Fest Ball committee. I just wanted to apologize for this evening. We, the committee that is, had no idea this rain would turn into a full-fledged nor'easter, or I assure you we would have rescheduled." I sugarcoated my voice as much as possible and reassured myself little white lies always sounded more believable with a pinch of sweetness.

Taglianno reached up and squeezed his wife's shoulder, giving her a comforting smile. "It's certainly no one's fault these disastrous events would all happen in one night. It's really a shame. What an unfortunate evening for you and the committee."

"Yes, and for Mr. Voorhees. He was so young. Just in his forties, I think."

"I wouldn't know. I didn't know the man."

"Oh, I must be mistaken. I thought I saw the two of you…in a…" I paused to be cautious about my word choice, "…*discussion* on the back deck a few hours ago."

Taglianno shifted in his seat, released his arm from around his wife and asked her to go get him a cup of coffee. She stood without question, only turning back once to give a worried look before she made her way into the kitchen. He turned to me. "I meant to say I didn't know him personally. We had business dealings a couple of times. That's all you saw was a business conversation, nothing else," he said, almost demanding I believe him. Then with a softening of his voice, he continued, "Of course, it's a terrible shame. I hope his wife will be okay."

I dreaded pressuring him. My fears stemmed from watching too many Mafia specials on A&E, but I slogged forward. "Yes, I was just going to check on her. Again, I hope this storm will end soon. If I can do anything to make you and your wife more comfortable until the road clears, please let me know." I left, wondering how seriously he took his business dealings, especially when they seemed so personal.

Turning, I noticed Barbara Voorhees's head bowed. She was conversing with other partygoers who were doing their best to console her. I feared I wouldn't get a chance to talk with her, however, for just as the rain and wind began to subside I heard a helicopter landing in the parking lot. Several emergency medical technicians and Lieutenant Mark Sherman from the Newport Police Department rushed through the door.

I recognized Sherman the moment he walked in. I had interviewed him a few times to get information for articles. He was congenial and helpful to a fault, sometimes even stepping over the boundaries of rigid police formality. I imagined his helpfulness stemmed more than anything else from a desire to see his name in print. Ego was a plus to me whenever I needed sensitive information.

Sherman with flashlight in hand, demanded to be led to the body immediately. He was pointed toward the chef's office, and charged off, EMTs in tow. I ran to catch him.

"Hi, Mark. I thought I should let you know we found his body at ten twenty-two, although it was around nine thirty, give or take, when he went back there to lie down." I paused to catch my breath before rushing on. "It could have been anyone. Lots of people already left before the bridge flooded."

"Which was when . . . and it's Morgan Langdon, right?" Mark asked, stopping in the hallway and holding up a hand, signaling the EMTs to do the same.

"Yes, it's good to see you again, but sorry it's under such circumstances. Let's see, I know the last crew to leave in the complimentary limo was a couple hours into the evening," I said, not certain of the exact time.

"I appreciate the info," he said. "Now you need to take me to him." Sherman flipped on his flashlight and I escorted him down the long hall to the office where the corpse lay.

The oil lamp Susan had carried into the room was still burning, its flickering light projecting shifting shadows onto the scene. From the doorway Sherman lifted his flashlight to shine a bright beam directly on the body. "Yep, I think we can rule out natural causes or suicide," he said, rolling his eyes. "Keep everyone out of here while I go back to the helicopter and get everything I need. I can see those extra classes in processing a murder scene will finally come in handy." He gave me his flashlight and looked me in the eye. "Keep everyone out and that includes you."

I nodded in compliance.

Nick was still standing guard at the end of the hall. I did as I was told and waited by the door. I could hear my heart pounding as I calmed myself by playing finger puppets on the wall with the flashlight. Being this near a murder victim was giving me the heebie-jeebies. I began remembering all the B-flick movies I'd watch as a teenager with titles like *Night of the Living Dead* and *Horror of the Zombies*. Those characters were fictional; this was all too real.

Shivers ran up my spine as my imagination ran wild. I had never checked his pulse. *Am I sure he's dead?* I pictured Voorhees standing up with the knife still in his back, eyes as black as coal, arms outstretched, walking toward me. I shook myself out of my momentary psychotic lapse. *Be professional and get a hold on yourself*, I told my shaking knees, just as a large cold hand touched my shoulder. I screamed and jumped like the soon-to-be-sacrificed ingénue in a chainsaw movie. I'd never live this one down as I turned and saw Mark giving me a crooked smile.

He set a bag of equipment outside the door and pulled thin blue booties over his shoes. He was inspecting his gear when he asked, "Do you have a camera? This one doesn't seem to be working. Maybe it's the battery. I don't know," he said exasperated.

"Sure, let me grab the club's." Within a minute I had returned with the camera, which earlier had taken pictures of happier subjects.

Slipping on latex gloves, he thanked me as he stepped onto the tile floor like a skater on thin ice, waving his flashlight across the floor in a slow methodical motion. Nothing was shouting evidence from my point of view, but then I wasn't an expert.

He taped, packaged, plucked, and fingerprinted everything possible. He photographed the room and body, up, down, and backward. Last to be handled was the extraction of the knife. He called in one of the EMTs who assessed the situation, called over the radio to a doctor at Newport General who pronounced Voorhees dead.

"Would you like to do the honors of extracting the knife?" Mark grinned at me.

"Oh, no. The EMT can have the honor," I said smirking at Mark. I watched, squinting my eyes. The room was as silent as a morgue after hours as he moved closer and leaned into Emile. Without notice the electricity flicked on and golden light filtered into the office. Cheers echoed down the hall. "Talk about divine intervention," I said, as I turned on the overhead light. Un-phased by the incident, the EMT gave a slight tug on the knife pulling it out with the precision of a surgeon. He slipped it into a plastic bag. There was less blood than I imagined there'd be.

"That seems to be about it. He's all yours," he said to the EMT. "I'm done in here." Mark waited to place "Do Not Enter" tape across the door until the stretcher was out of view. "I'm not going to release the crime scene until I get this information processed. I'm going to need to confiscate your camera card and get a key to this joint."

I felt a slight panic. "Mark, now that we have electricity, would you mind if I printed off the pictures from the ball? I took so many. I'd hate to lose them to a novice disorganized lab tech." My true motive was a bit more devious.

"I'm still going to need the card. Our murderer could be on there somewhere. But okay, just hurry up about it."

"Great. I'll be as quick as a bunny."

He looked up at the ceiling rolling his eyes. "I'll be in the ballroom after I check out the rest of the facility," he said.

Jogging into the secretary's office, I kept my fingers crossed, hoping there would be enough photo paper. I searched the storage unit under the printer. *Yes!* I pumped my fist. I popped the picture card into the printer, flipped it on, pushed a few buttons and voila! Technology was wonderful when you knew how to use it. I dashed back to the dance floor stealthily sliding one set of murder scene photos into my purse as I grabbed the keys to the club.

I noticed that the music had now been replaced with the hum of voices. The harsh overhead lighting and grizzly circumstances had doused the last flicker of romantic ambience and the rain had finally ceased. I was still hopeful for Frank and Carol, however, when I spotted them in the far corner, looking out the window and engaged in an intimate conversation. My subconscious patted my mental back for one thing gone right this evening.

Mark, with pad and pen in hand, was asking routine questions of everyone lucid enough to speak. Where were you after nine thirty? Did you know the victim? How long have you been a member? I only caught the tail end of some of the interrogations. He got everyone's name, license plates, and telephone numbers, then motioned me to the front door where I handed him the camera card, keys, and one set of photos. I knew at some point Mark would forgive my subterfuge. For now I would keep quiet.

"It seems clear-cut how he died, but a formal autopsy will still be performed. If no one needs immediate assistance, we'll evacuate the body. I'll be back later to do a thorough investigation of the area." Mark motioned for the EMTs to roll the body out as quickly as they could. The storm had lifted and the tide was going out. Sherman seemed to think the bridge would soon be passable. He ran to the helicopter clambering over the skids where the body was placed. The engine whirred as it propelled debris around in a circular motion. Lifting off, the craft and its occupants flew into the pitch-black darkness.

I watched from the front door as Sherman disappeared into the night air. Mrs. Voorhees was still seated. She had declined Mark's invitation to go along with the body in the helicopter. If that were Nick, I wouldn't leave his side, dead or alive.

I kept my face down, feeling lost, when Nick rounded the corner and ran square into me. "Hey, honey. Look what I found—an extra serving of tiramisu. Want some?" He swallowed a huge bite of chocolate whipped cream and brandied ladyfingers. I felt enjoying oneself after a murder seemed a bit crass, except when it came to dessert.

I bit off the piece Nick had proffered me on his fork. The flavors mingled in my mouth and made my brain, for an instant, forget the task at hand. I swallowed saying, "Would you stop enticing me? I've got work to do."

"We've already had this conversation," he said. "It's one thing to investigate puppy mills and quite another to go poking into a murder. This is not a piece you need to concern yourself with."

I knew he couldn't have forgotten my major investigative effort to date. "How can you be so cavalier? You know about the arguments we overheard tonight. And then there's his wife who hasn't shed a tear. Don't you think all these 'coincidences,' " I said, raising my hands in the air and fingering quotation marks, "add up to quite a few guilty parties?"

Irritated Nick said, "Okay, Miss Marple, if you insist on creating controversy, who am I to stop you? But for now we need to check on the road and see if it's safe to drive so we can get everyone home."

I had to agree. "You take the SUV and go check. I'll make sure everything gets closed and locked." I kissed him and told him to be careful. The door opened. I breathed in the still, humid air of the calm after the storm. Looking up I imagined I could see the moon trying to peek its ethereal face through the clearing night sky.

The committee members converged upon the registration table. They realized we had forgotten about the raffle tickets for the wreath-and-lamp centerpieces. Without any fanfare they pulled the winners from a large glass bowl. One of them was Barbara Voorhees.

Sensitive to the circumstances, Carol asked, "Do you want me to wait and give this to her at a later date?"

Realizing the timing couldn't have come at a worse moment, I made a suggestion. "Let's just leave them all here for now. I can take Barbara's to her after the funeral. She might enjoy the distraction at that point." I looked at Carol. "Maybe you and Frank can deliver the others." Internally I was wringing my hands like an evil scientist. My suggestion wasn't as altruistic as it sounded. My motive was twofold. One, delivering the flowers could help give Carol and Frank some needed time together; and two, in the process of delivering Barbara Voorhees's prize, I might be able to answers some of the questions that were floating around in my everyone-is-guilty-until-proven-innocent mind. All agreed.

Nick came in and announced as loudly as he could that crossing the bridge was now safe. The DJ had already packed up his paraphernalia. After blowing out all the lamps, Art let the kitchen crew go with everyone else. He said the night had already been too long. The workers would return tomorrow or as soon as the police allowed, to finish cleaning up the remnants of plates left scattered about. Then everyone piled into their cars and the limo in a great mass exodus. Nick took Barbara Voorhees by the arm and led her outside to the only Mercedes left in the lot. He insisted on driving her home, I agreed and would follow.

Before leaving I took a backward glance across the empty dance floor. Through the windows I could see Newport illuminated in the distance. I flicked off the last light as a faint roll of thunder moved across the early morning sky and a cold indeterminate chill rippled down my spine.

CHAPTER 5

Sunday, October 6

It could have been a perfect Sunday morning with the sun's rays piercing through the early morning clouds as Cooper and I finished a brisk walk around the block. But it wasn't, because the terror of the previous night was just now sinking in. I unhooked Cooper from his leash at the bottom of the driveway. Nick and I had grabbed only a few hours of sleep, but our late night did nothing to alter Cooper's internal time clock or bladder. He stood staring and panting on the back porch while, like a slug, I made my way toward him and flung open the screened door. I'm sure he was wondering what took me so long. I dropped the leash on the kitchen floor and dragged myself down the hall to our bedroom. It was a bit before eight o'clock and I was sleep deprived. I found Nick awake and propped up with all the pillows piled behind him.

I leaned over and ruffled his bed head. He was about to reciprocate the love rub when a big ball of fur jumped up and landed on the sports section scattered between Nick's legs. The mug of coffee dangling by a few fingers over the edge of the bed dribbled onto the cartoon section below as Cooper landed a big wet one on Nick's cheek.

"Thanks, buddy," Nick said, wiping away the slobber. "Why are you up so early?" he asked me. "Cooper could have held it in for a bit longer. Besides, church doesn't start for a few hours." Nick shooed the dog off the paper.

"I could ask the same thing. You were fast asleep when we left. Now you're awake with coffee. Impressive."

"I dreamed you were kidnapped by the Mafia and I was trying to save you, but I got hoisted overboard with a lead balloon. I woke up right as I was taking my last breath. I decided sleep wasn't all that important. I'll take a nap this afternoon."

"Sorry to hear you didn't sleep well, but thanks for trying to save me. Ah, love even transcends the conscious mind."

"Back to my original question. Were you having nightmares too? Or are you planning on coming back to bed?" He patted the mattress and grinned.

"Imagine if we're feeling this way how awful it will be for Art and his crew. I think they could use a bit of help. Those employees shouldn't have to work on a Sunday, especially after the events of last night."

"Aren't you the Saint of Helpfulness? Besides, didn't they tape off the crime scene? We're probably not allowed in there, yet."

"There's no need for mockery. Besides, I've already talked to Mark."

"Of course you have. I wouldn't have expected anything less." He was making fun of me I knew, but ignoring him could be one of my strong suits when I needed it to be.

"Yes, and his crew showed up not long after we left this morning. They took care of perimeter evidence, you know, inside the ballroom, kitchen, and around the outside of the building. So the only room that will be off limits is Art's office." I breathed a sigh of guess-I'll-get-my-way-after-all, breath. Nick sighed annoyance.

I picked up the remnants of the paper and flipped through until I arrived at the obituaries. "Hey look here. That was quick. Voorhees death *is* listed." I skimmed down over the paragraph. "Just says he died at the yacht club under suspicious circumstances. They probably want to keep the details hush-hush for as long as they can. Let's see, it says he owned a few successful jewelry stores called Beauty by Design. His wife is only surviving family member. Hmm."

"What's that *hmm* about? What else are you up to?" Nick's piqued curiosity was revealed in his partially upturned lip.

"I have no idea what you're insinuating."

"Oh, brother. You're not really going to help out. You're going to the club to *in-ves-ti-gate*, aren't you, Miss Marple, even though it's obvious that Mark wants to keep this quiet? And has Bob, your editor, called you yet? Don't answer. That's a rhetorical question." Exasperated, Nick jumped out of bed and threw off his bathrobe. "I might as well go with you. I can check on the boat and make sure it weathered the storm while you play house detective. Meet you in the shower in ten minutes."

I obliged. I loved Sunday mornings and shared showers.

A police vehicle and one officer greeted us at the door reminding us to stay away from the crime scene. We obliged entering into the yacht club. The officer followed and headed down the hall. Cooper dashed inside. I was certain my handsome shepherd appreciated the intensity of the situation and was just as eager as I was to sniff out clues. The smells from last night's dinner still lingered in the air.

"It doesn't look like anyone else has been here yet," I said to Nick, locking the door behind me.

"Why would they? Who in their right mind would be here this early after such a dreadful night? Oh, wait, I know, the Caped Crusader of Investigative Reporting."

"You certainly are grumpy without a second cup of coffee, aren't you?" I threw my jacket over a chair and walked to the place where the Voorheeses were last seated. I maneuvered around the table stopping halfway to peer at the emptiness of the table. I expected to see plates and half-filled glasses because the kitchen crew hadn't had time to clean up all of the tables before the lights went out. They had begun nearest the kitchen but had stopped when we heard Barbara's blood curdling scream. I turned back to the table and scratched the side of my head.

"What are you seeing?"

"It's funny. Voorhees's table is the only one that appears cleared on this side of the room. I could have sworn when I sat Barbara down that it hadn't been cleaned off."

"Maybe the kitchen crew started cleaning by lamplight after things calmed down?"

"Maybe, but they had started at that end being so methodical. Why skip over to here?" My absorption of the details made me jump when Cooper barked his intruder warning. I heard a key turning in the front door lock. "Stay, Cooper." Nick and I turned to see whose face would clear the doorway to the entry hall. It was Art. He strode in with a look of surprise on his face as he was met with a sniff and a gruff from Cooper.

"Hello. I wasn't expecting anyone to be here yet." He looked down and patted Cooper on the head. "You do know some of the kitchen staff will be coming in this afternoon. I don't want you to think I'm letting them shirk their responsibilities. Has anyone else been here?"

Nick, who was still half-asleep, said, "Oh no, just us eager helpful beavers."

I slapped Nick on the shoulder. "You'll have to excuse him. He's not himself without half a gallon of coffee."

"I can fix that," Art said. "I'll put on a pot. I hate to see anyone go without their early morning jolt, especially when they're volunteering for cleanup duty." He headed through the double doors that led to the kitchen. I could hear him shuffling coffee pots and mugs around on the stainless steel countertop.

"I suppose now that I'm getting coffee I'll have to help pick up?"

"You could share the Saint of Helpfulness title if you did." I said, batting my eyelashes in his direction. "Let's start with the centerpieces and put them by the front door so I don't forget to take them home. I'll get Frank and Carol to help hand deliver them later this week."

"Is this another effort of yours to play Cupid?"

I held to the belief that a silent response was like a picture: it could paint a thousand words.

Fifteen minutes passed before Art emerged from the back with a tray. It held a white, insulated coffee pot, sugar and creamer. He plopped the tray onto the mahogany bar and began pouring. The heady aroma of coffee wafted through the air, bringing an abrupt halt to our manual labor. Nick and I made our way to the cushioned barstools. We each grabbed a mug and added the required substances to make it perfect. In my case, that meant at least a couple teaspoons of sugar and plenty of cream.

I held the ten grams of creamy fat in both hands as if it were a dear friend I hadn't seen in years and began sipping the warm liquid. Cooper walked over and placed a paw on my leg. I had made the mistake one day of letting him lick my coffee mug clean and now he thought the task was his duty. I gestured the command for him to lie down and wait as I leaned into the high-backed stool, enjoying any moments I could spend with my two favorite males.

For the second time that morning there was a bark and a whoosh of glass doors.

"What are *you* doing here?" I said, astonished to see Susan out so early.

"I could ask you the same thing."

I blushed, more from guilt than from embarrassment. I would never let on that my main purpose was to play *I Spy* before anyone else had a chance. "Nick was concerned about the boat and wanted to make sure it didn't get knocked about too much from the storm," I replied. "And I needed to pick up the centerpieces. Why don't you join us for coffee?"

"A hot cup of coffee sounds good. There's a nip in the air. I suppose one cup won't hurt before I go check on my boat." Susan pulled up a stool and poured herself a cup of black coffee, something I couldn't imagine savoring.

My eagerness to pursue a deadly perpetrator was subsiding as another cup of the smooth liquid rolled around in my mouth and down my throat. Starting a conversation, I hoped, would head off any work until we had to leave for Sunday service. Not that I would ever admit that to Nick. "Art, how did you decide to settle in Harbor View?"

He reflected a moment then answered. "A few reasons I suppose. I was tired of owning my own business. I wanted to make a regular paycheck without all of the headaches that come from earning it. Although there have been moments with this job when I've felt like I never left Boston. You own your own business; you must know how that feels." He gave me a dad smile.

"Oh, yes. I love what I do, but there are a lot of headaches in ownership. Sometimes it's nice to just be an employee. So what else brought you this direction?"

"I suppose I wanted a change of scenery. The Boston area reminded me too often of the tragic accident that killed my wife, Betty, and my daughter, Charlene." Everyone shifted. Death was never a comfortable subject. "We called her Charley. She used to tease us, saying we called her that because we were never blessed with a son, so she had to play both roles. That couldn't have been further from the truth. From the time she was born until she emerged as a beautiful young woman, she fulfilled all of our parenting dreams."

I could see the prideful sorrow in his eyes as he stared out the windows, past the moored boats to the ocean in the distance. Shaking off the past he said, "Anyway, we used to vacation on the Rhode Island coast every year and do touristy things like visiting the Newport mansions. This area brings back happy memories. It wasn't a difficult decision on where to move and it was my good luck that the yacht club was hiring."

Although I was more curious than a cat at a mouse hole, I knew when to steer clear, especially where heartache was concerned. "I can tell you with confidence that the committee is glad you took the head chef position. You've done a great job. I'm sure there won't be any more nights like last night."

"Oh, I'm quite certain there won't be," Art replied.

Susan had been sipping her coffee, seemingly aloof to the conversation. I hadn't known her for very long and I wondered if her distracted demeanor was genuine contemplation of another's feelings or if her innate coldness and insensitivity were showing through. Maybe, just maybe, the death of her estranged lover was having more impact on her than I imagined. I chose to believe the best and placed a hand on Susan's shoulder.

"How are you holding up? I know as a doctor you probably see death more than the rest of us, but it still can't be easy. You were close."

Susan set her mug down and slipped off her seat. "Art, can you grab me a bottle of your driest chardonnay and put it on my tab, please?" He pulled one from the refrigerator below. She thanked him, grabbing her jacket. Then without agreeing or disagreeing with my comment, she said, "I need to get going and check on my boat. Maybe I'll see you out there later." She made her way across the floor, opened the back door and disappeared down the walk toward the docks.

"Susan's right, honey. We need to finish what we came to do. I'll go check on *Irish Eyes* if you want to finish up here."

"Okay. I'll help Art until you're done checking the boat. Then I'll meet you at the car."

The coffee had kicked in and stirred my complacent attitude. I recalled that the big reason why I had gone to the club early was to see if I had missed anything of importance the night before.

I pondered if Nick may be right to a certain degree; perhaps murder isn't my thing. If only there wasn't this itching at the back of my spine that kept me scratching for answers.

I set down my mug, stretched and yawned. Jumping off my stool, I said, "Art, do you know if anyone cleared off the Voorheeses' table last night?"

"Not that I know of. After the lights went out and…well, everything else…I told the crew not to worry about anything until this afternoon. Why?"

"I thought it odd that their table was cleared but none of the others on this side of the room were."

"Oh. Maybe some of the staff thought she'd be more comfortable with a clean table. Why? Is it important?"

I smiled, shaking my head. "No. I'm sure it isn't." But I didn't believe my own words. "Is there anything else I can do for you before I take those out to the car?" I pointed to the pile of wreaths and lamps lying near the front entrance.

“No thanks. I’ll be fine. As I said, I’ll have plenty of help later on. Have a good day. I’m sure I’ll be seeing you around.”

“I’m sure you will. Thanks for the coffee. It was delicious.” Picking up a few wreaths, I called Cooper over and made him sit so I could place two of them around his neck. I patted him on the head and grabbed a few more to sling over my arm and we headed out the door.

Later that morning on the drive home from church, instead of contemplating the sermon I imagined myself in a conversation with Barbara Voorhees. I asked her about her relationship with her husband. I wondered if her detached attitude the night before was from the shock of murder or from a heart that had been hardened during many years of a bad marriage. Worse yet, maybe hers was an attitude of revenge completed. I was determined to find where the truth lay, one way or another.

CHAPTER 6

A routine autopsy had been performed. The lab work was still being processed. Emile Voorhees's body was put to rest in a small cemetery in upstate Connecticut where he was born and raised. The funeral came and went without much ceremony. Only a handful of people attended, including Nick and me. Susan lingered nearby under a tree until everyone had said their last words and filed away in their cars. Then she approached the casket and placed one red rose upon the carved mahogany before smiling and strolling away.

Saturday, October 12

Exactly one week had passed since the Fall Fest Ball. I had already invited Frank and Carol over to pick up the centerpieces and I insisted they go together to deliver all but one. I was sure, from the looks I received, that they were skeptical of my motives, but they obliged nevertheless.

I decided to give Mark a call and see if he had heard anything that could further my award-winning story. "Hi, Mark. This is Morgan Langdon. You're a tough guy to get hold of at the office."

"What can I tell you? I'm a busy guy and there's lots of crime."

"Sorry to hear that. In regards to crime, however, have you got any news about the Voorhees case that could sway the direction my story is taking?"

"Probably more than you think. It may have seemed obvious that Voorhees died from a stab wound, but that's not what the coroner is saying. Do you remember…there was very little blood around the wound?"

I didn't give Mark a chance to continue. I wanted to show him I was on the forensic ball. "Of course. With little blood then there was no circulation going on, which means he was already dead. Right?"

"That's right, Miss Smarty-pants. The blood and tissue samples have been tested. I have to tell you that the coroner, from the preliminary results, is saying it was a heart attack. But they're sending samples to toxicology and it could take some time, they have quite a backlog. For now the report for the paper will be he died under suspicious circumstances. Given what we know, we can't charge anyone with murder because he was already dead when the knife went into him—although we will be required to find the person who stabbed him. They could possibly be charged with intent to murder, not on what actually happened. Besides, the chief already handed these facts to the papers, so although the circumstances are confusing, in the final analysis, for now, we have nothing."

"You don't believe it was just a heart attack, do you?"

"The evidence speaks for itself, until we hear otherwise. Listen, I have to go. Some sailboats at the dock have been broken into. I need to get down there."

"Sure. May I call you later?"

"No problem."

I hung up the phone. I knew my subconscious was trying to tell me something. There's no way this death was from natural causes. I was certain they would find something else, but what and when was the question. My instincts were never wrong. Well, almost never. Nick's mom was notorious for popping in unannounced. I was certain she would show her face on our anniversary weekend. She loved surprising me with tasty hot meals knowing I'm not the greatest cook.

Once we hadn't seen her for at least a month and she called asking what our plans were for the weekend. Women's intuition screamed, scrub the house to perfection. Order something from Fago's, the one gourmet restaurant in town, and pretend you cooked it. But she never showed. What a surprise it should not have been when she showed up the following weekend when I had four loads of laundry piled up, wet dog towels lying about from Cooper's afternoon bath and dirty dishes in the sink from a get-together the night before. *Argh.* I suppose when it comes to a mother-in-law with a name like Lauren Lucille Langdon, one can never know for sure what will happen.

I decided today would be my day to visit Barbara Voorhees. I felt I had waited an appropriate amount of time. Besides, if I had to bounce off the walls one more day, Cooper and my husband were going to make me live on the boat. I had called her the day before to ask how she was doing. Then with fox like precision I invited myself to her home.

Cooper and I went into work earlier than usual Saturday morning to organize paperwork and to make sure Jessica showed up on time. Ten in the morning seemed like early afternoon to me since I was always up by six, but anything before eleven was difficult for Jessica. I think she is part vampire, at least in her sleep habits.

The big hand on my dog clock moved to the number ten and it chimed a Chihuahua yap. I should have become accustomed by this time to hearing the different dogs barks mark the hour, but no such luck. I still jumped whenever the German shepherd woofed nine o'clock because it sounded much like Cooper in defense mode. My favorite bark was the hound dog at two o'clock. It reminded my of the neighbor's hunting dog, Sam, for whom I always felt sorry. The dog was caged for weeks on end until the owners decided they wanted to go hunting. It didn't take me long to persuade Mr. Miller to let me walk his dog on a weekly basis. Sam and I became great pals those few summers we had together, although on occasion he'd dragged me through the mud whenever he caught a glimpse of a squirrel. Then it was all I could do to hold on for dear life until the little critter scampered up a tree. I had somehow forgotten the cardinal rule of letting go of the leash after you fall on your face.

At the last yip of the chime, Jessica flung herself through the door. "Bet ya thought I forgot to wake up this morning?"

"The thought had crossed my mind. But now that you're here, listen up. Cooper and I are going to visit some of the residents of the Maple Grove Nursing Home this morning. Then I'll be visiting Mrs. Voorhees this afternoon in case you need to reach me on my cell phone."

"Voorhees? Isn't that the guy whose lights went out at your party last week?"

"Literally, in a word, yes. So unless it's an emergency, please don't call. Okay?"

"Okay. Hey, do you want to hear last night's short story reading?" Before I had a chance to think up an excuse, Jessica was off and running about how she was going to become a female Jack Kerouac. This frightened me. I never did understand Kerouac, even in college.

"I think my story really embodies the American sexual paradox," Jessica said.

Catching my breath and halting any further discussion on that topic, I interjected, "Great, just hold that thought and go with it while you stock the shelves with this new shipment that came in yesterday," I said, pointing to five large boxes stacked beside the counter. "I'll be back at three."

Hanging up her jacket and throwing her backpack behind the counter, she smiled, apparently taking no offense at my shortness. "You and Cooper make lots of smiles today and good luck with the stiff's wife."

I shook my head and prayed that Jessica wasn't always that blunt with my customers as I grabbed some treats off the shelf and made a mental note to take them off the inventory list.

The nursing home visit went off without a hitch. Cooper was always a big hit. As usual I heard a plethora of stories about people's pets from fifty years ago. Many of the tales were repeats from past visits, like the one Mrs. Sotheby told. She and her husband once owned a police dog just like Cooper. I noticed the older generation always equated shepherds with police work. One day her husband was out chopping wood with a chainsaw and their dear Duke got in the way and off came his back leg like it was a twig on a branch. Then, in reminiscing, Mrs. Sotheby would get teary-eyed until Cooper placed his paw on her lap. She would pat him on the head and call me dearie as she thanked us for coming to visit. This particular scene had occurred so many times I knew the whole story by heart.

Driving to Barbara Voorhees's house I sporadically looked at the directions I had scribbled on a scrap of paper the day before. Although Nick and I had driven her home after the ball, the night had been dark and I hadn't really paid attention to where we drove. I checked my notes again. *Is it two lights then a left, or left at the second light?* I now wished I had entered the address into my navigational system before I'd begun driving, but I was determined to become less directionally challenged, so I ignored the small screen on my dashboard.

After one wrong turn and a few bangs on the steering wheel from my fist, I drove up the cobblestone, circle-shaped driveway. It entered and exited at the same point and in the middle stood a landscaped island with a stone fountain. I stopped parallel to the entrance of the large, gray, Federal-style house. I loved all architectural styles, but this one was a particular favorite. Federal style was always symmetrical with a calm, uninterrupted flow. The six-over-six, double-hung windows projected an image of grace with minimal ornamentation, somewhat like Barbara herself.

The day was cool, but clear. I left Cooper napping in the back seat while I grabbed the box with the centerpiece and made my way to the dark-green wooden entryway. I turned the manual door chime and waited to hear signs of life inside. They came in the form of a pint-sized bark. Barbara Voorhees opened the door, hushing the Muppet-sized pooch as she invited me into the expansive airy hallway. She was dressed casually in tan corduroys, her white linen shirt un-tucked. She seemed to be more at ease with herself than I had seen her before and I wondered if death normally had that affect. She stretched out an arm, inviting me to the parlor on the right. We entered through the double pocket doors and sat on a silk settee that faced an orange marble fireplace.

"I started a fire. I thought the air seemed a bit chilly this morning."

"It's very cozy in here." I paused, taking in the earthy smell of the burning wood. "I'm so glad you were up to having company."

She nodded but made no reply.

I reached down and scratched the small dog under the chin. "I remember you from my pet store," I said. "You're Cocoa, the Papillon, and you love dried liver treats." I reached into my pocket and pulled one out. The small nose reached forward and licked it first before extracting it from my hand.

"You have a great memory for names," Barbara said.

Red-faced I admitted, "That's only true with pet names. I'm terrible at remembering human names."

"That's a beneficial quality in someone who owns a pet store. I'm sure most of your customers find that very charming. Would you like some tea?" Barbara picked up a china teapot from the coffee table and held the top while she poured. Both of her pinky fingers dangled away from her other digits, revealing her status as a most refined hostess.

"Please." Nodding yes to sugar and a little milk, I leaned over and picked up what I considered my peace offering before I launched into my investigative questioning.

"I hope this isn't in bad taste to bring you this centerpiece. Your ticket was pulled the evening of the ball. Of course we never had the chance to present the centerpieces to the winners because of the storm and…" I stumbled to find a word that would be appropriate.

"You were going to say murder, I know. But according to Lieutenant Sherman, who told me not to worry, Emile more than likely died from heart problems; which really doesn't shock me," she said. "I'm certain that's what they'll find out in the end. I'm glad for that, and not just for the obvious reasons. I don't think I could have handled an investigation. All the questions and prying would have been too much. I'm putting the whole worrisome night out of my head. Just like Scarlett, I'll think about it tomorrow."

As she paused to take a sip of tea I had to remove my chin from my lap. Was this a normal attitude for such a repulsive act of violence on someone you supposedly loved? Indeed it may be a heart attack when all is said and done, but he was still stabbed no matter how you spin it.

"Thank you, though, for bringing this by," she continued. "They were quite pretty when they were all lit up on the tables." She caressed the berries on the wreath. "The night of the party we arrived late because Emile had just gotten off work. He had such long days and was looking forward to dinner and dancing." She paused, looking into the fire. "It's such a shame. You did a wonderful job decorating."

I wanted to interject, *you're the one who wanted to dance, not him,* but I thought better of it. "Thanks, I can't take all of the credit. We had a committee," I said. "You may know some of them. There was Carol Smith and Diane Handers, they're from Harbor View. And Frank Broward, he lives with his mother right off Bellevue Avenue. And Susan Fairfield, she's a cardiologist at Newport General." I waited for signs of recognition or even an admission she knew Susan, but Barbara was as artful in her coyness as Monet was in his Impressionism.

"Yes, I do believe I've heard of Frank Broward's mother. She comes from old money from what I hear."

"True, she's loaded, but that doesn't mean she has an ounce of class. She can drink as much as a herd of cattle lost in the desert, and she treats her son like he's hired help." Immediately embarrassed by my bluntness, I apologized. "I certainly don't want to start any rumors about Amanda Broward and her drinking habits."

"No need to apologize. I was there last Saturday night; I saw firsthand how she held her liquor *and* her mothering techniques. I suppose it doesn't matter how old children are, parents can still manage to make them feel like they're ten years old again. It's all so sad. One's children should be a blessing."

"I agree. Nick and I haven't had any children yet, but we'd like to someday. How about you? Did you and Emile ever have children?"

"No, Emile was always too concerned with establishing his businesses. He owns, I mean owned, a few jewelry stores called Beauty by Design. Maybe you've heard of them?"

"I've seen your billboards, but have never been shopping in one."

Barbara looked away from me and poured herself another cup of tea. "We started in Boston with one store and then another on the other side of the city. A year ago we opened one in Newport. That's when we decided to move. The pace here is slower and quieter."

There was momentary silence while we sipped. "I know what you mean about a slower pace. The traffic is hideous in Boston. Nick and I love Harbor View. We're still close to the city but without all of the headaches. It's a plus too that my mom and dad live in Compton where I grew up, so anywhere in Rhode Island is home to me. Where are you from originally?"

Lifting her Wedgwood teacup to her rose-colored lips, she said haughtily, "Why Newport, of course. I was born and raised here. My father is Theodore Dinsforth III, great-great nephew of the Vanderbilts."

"Oh, I see. I had no idea." Her revelation meant about as much to me as the stock exchange page in the Sunday paper. "Then I guess I could assume it was your money that gave Emile his start with Beauty by Design?"

I always thought I could have been a protégé to Lesley Stahl on *60 Minutes*. I loved asking the tough emotional questions and then watching the body language and retorts that followed.

Shifting on the damask-covered settee, Barbara Voorhees laid down her teacup and looked straight into my eyes. "My dowry may have helped start the business, but its success was Emile's business sense. He was a very hard worker who never let anything distract him from his goals."

I wondered if Barbara knew that some of those goals were extramarital affairs, but I thought it best to keep the facts to myself, at least for now. "I didn't mean to imply he wasn't successful. I'm just assuming it takes quite a bit of collateral to start such an expensive venture."

"Yes, it does." She obviously knew how to play the game of chess. "You own a retail store in Harbor View, so what does your husband do for a living? I'm sure starting a pet store in a lovely tourist village like Harbor View must have required quite a down payment."

Touché, I thought. *I like her.* "Nick's a dentist in Harbor View. He's been in practice almost seven years, and my pet store well…I had been saving since college. When we found the building we're in now, it needed a lot of TLC, but a pet shop of my own has been a dream since childhood. I can't say I'm as business savvy as others, but the store does pretty well for itself."

Picking up Cocoa, Barbara stroked the dog's fur and said, "We both thought it was quite inviting. I'm sure we'll be back."

"Thanks very much. I want people to feel comfortable. You know, bring their pets in, walk around, and check things out. In fact my dog Cooper comes to work with me everyday. That's one of the great perks of being your own boss. He's out in the car right now." I looked out the paned windows to the driveway.

"We should go out and say hello. What kind of dog is he?"

"He's a German shepherd named after my grandpa. He looks intimidating, but he's really a big teddy bear."

Barbara lowered Cocoa into a chenille-pillowed wicker basket. The Papillon turned around three times on the soft fabric and then lay down and shut her eyes. We walked outside under the portico, which was flanked on either side by large white columns. We paused; then stepped down to the driveway. Cooper stood up, wagged his tail and pushed his face out the partially opened window to greet us.

"He's quite a handsome fellow. I'm sure you feel safe with him around."

"I suppose I do, but thankfully he's never had a chance to show his true colors. I sometimes think he would lick a burglar to death before he would bite."

"Oh, you never know. The handsome, calm types can sometimes pack quite a bite if they have the opportunity."

Her words trailed off to some unknown place and I wondered if Barbara were talking about dogs or men. Not wanting to lose any momentum in the conversation, I asked, "So, what do you think will happen to Beauty by Design? Will you take over running the businesses?"

"I know nothing about jewelry or what it takes to run a business. It was Emile's dream, not mine. I suppose I'll sell the stores. I'm not sure."

Here was my chance to let the cat out of the bag. I was almost certain Barbara knew nothing about Emile's run-in with the Mafia man last Saturday evening. However, I was quite certain she wasn't as naïve in the business world as she pretended. "How do you think you'll handle the Taglianno problem?"

With as much grace as she had used to pour tea, she turned and with the back of her hand she brushed some dog hair from her shoulder. "Taglianno? The name sounds familiar, but I'm not sure what problem you're speaking about." Looking into my eyes with a blank stare, then up to the house, she said, "Shall we go back inside? I feel a chill?"

I knew this wasn't a suggestion; it was a polite command to keep my nosy interference in check. I patted Cooper and followed Barbara back inside. I knew there wasn't much chance I could get any further with her today. Ending the conversation on a positive, complimentary note might be just the ticket to be invited back. I hoped.

"Nick doesn't purchase jewelry for me. His taste doesn't go beyond the costume jewelry at the local department store. I'd love to visit your place in Newport. What are the hours?"

"I'm not certain, but I do have some store information. Just a moment, I'll go and get it for you." She exited and disappeared through a door at the end of the hallway and reappeared a moment later with a business card in hand. "Here you go. It lists all of the stores and their telephone numbers. I'm sure you can call and they'll give you whatever information you need."

"Thanks so much. I'll try to stop by your Newport store next week and let you know if I splurged on anything. Have a good afternoon." I grabbed my purse and jacket and let myself out. Jumping into the Volvo I smelled the odor of *parfume de dirty dog.* "Dog bath first, buddy, before jewelry shopping." I knew I'd love dreaming over the diamonds and sapphires, but what I really hoped for was some clue to lead me to a perpetrator who just might be getting away with murder.

CHAPTER 7

Sunday, October 13

Bells chimed in the tall white steeple telling the towns people that Sunday services had ended. The sermon for the day had been titled, "Death Can Be a Blessing." I thought the title apropos for the week's events and wondered how many people felt Mr. Voorhees's death was a blessing.

I leaned over my afternoon lunch of chili con carne. With elbows straddling the bowl I pulled my cable-knit sweater closer to my chin and contemplated taking another bite. I wasn't sure if the chill I was feeling was coming from the partially opened back screen door or the troublesome images popping into my brain. The one thing I've learned when investigating stories is that there are very few coincidences in life. I was hard-pressed to believe Emile died from natural causes when at least a few people, if not one in particular, appeared to want him out of the picture. I wasn't about to wait around for the wheels of bureaucracy to turn.

"Say, let's go down to the boat this afternoon and do some winterizing. I can take some hot chocolate and munchies. It'll be fun," I said to Nick, hoping my motives weren't totally transparent.

They were. "I suppose the possibility of running into anyone who was at the party last weekend never crossed your mind?" Nick responded.

"You are such a suspicious person. I just want some quality time with my adorable husband and our four-legged companion." I whisked the plates and bowls off the table and into the farmhouse sink.

"Hey, I wasn't finished. Bring that back here." He raised his spoon in the air and grabbed another piece of pumpernickel bread with his free hand. "I'll go, but I want to finish my bowl of chili first."

I kissed the top of his head and acquiesced. "Great. I'll get some things together while you finish."

Large billowing clouds filled the sky as Nick and I grabbed bags out of the back of the car. Cooper knew just where he was going. In his excitement he had already jumped out the door and raced ahead of us and down the dock to where our boat was slipped. The club had four piers and each pier held sixteen boats, eight on each side. The first one was for smaller vessels, ones under twenty feet or so. The others were all reserved for the larger sailboats and some motorboats. We were at slip forty-eight, the last slip on dock three. That location made for easy access in and out. We could maneuver *Irish Eyes* effortlessly into her slip. The only negative was that our slip wasn't as close to the parking lot and club as most of the others were. By the time we lugged all our gear on board we usually needed to flop down into the cockpit to relax for a moment. Such was the case this day. Although the weather was cool and the days growing shorter, the leaves had not yet fallen. Blazing shades of amber and red in the trees created a spectacular view across the bay.

We had fashioned a special gangplank for Cooper so he could access the boat from the pier whenever he wanted, but most days he chose to run up and down the dock greeting everyone. I unscrewed the thermos of steaming hot chocolate and poured two mugs as Nick and I rocked to the rhythm of the waves.

"It's pretty quiet around here. I wonder if anyone will go sailing today to enjoy the scenery. It's quite a setting with all those deep hues mingling together. It reminds me of a Thomas Kinkade painting," he said.

"Aren't we poetic this afternoon? I never knew you could be so introspective. It makes you even cuter than before." Nick raised his eyebrows, smiled and lifted his mug in salute.

Just as we were thinking we would be the only ones enjoying the perfect fall day, Cooper announced a visitor with a loud happy bark. Susan came strolling out of the yacht club, carrying a basketful of cleaning supplies. She ignored Cooper and boarded her twenty-five foot Watkins she had named *Resuscitate*. I assumed this was a double entendre; after all she was in cardiology, but sailing can certainly revitalize a person emotionally and physically.

"Aye, neighbor," I called across the small expanse of water that separated the two docks. "We were wondering when someone else would show up. What are you up to today?"

Susan was slipped in fifty-one, far enough away that a casual conversation would have to be spoken loudly. She didn't respond. She just waved, flipped on her radio, and went to work on her boat.

"I think I'll take a jaunt over and see if she needs any help. Want to come along?" I was already ambling across Cooper's homemade platform and down the dock before Nick realized he even had a say in the matter. Cooper tagged along beside me, an old rope dangling from his mouth. "Cooper you stay." I held my flattened hand up in the air to signify he needed to stay put. "I'll be right back," I said, pulling my jacket around my ears.

I leaned against a pylon jutting from the fourth dock. The wind had kicked up a notch, rolling the boat and causing

Susan to grab her boom to steady herself. "Hi. Just thought I'd come over and see if you needed help with anything."

"I've been doing this by myself for a few years now. I think I can handle it. Thanks anyway," Susan said with such a self-confident, go-away tone. This might have kept a more sensitive person at a distance, but her message didn't stop me. I had ulterior motives and was as determined in my quest as Frodo Baggins in pursuit of a ring.

"Then I'll just keep you company for a bit."

Susan rolled her eyes and ignored my perkiness. I gave her a hearty grin and heaved myself on board.

"It's hard to believe it's been over a week since the Fall Fest Ball." I moved the jib line out of the way to sit, pausing for a reply, but none came. "I went to visit Barbara Voorhees yesterday. She seems to be holding up quite well for a woman who just buried her husband—and under such dreadful circumstances too."

This solicited a momentary glance from Susan, who was busy placing the rope back into a perfect concentric circle. I wasn't sure what the look implied until she spoke.

"I would think she would be holding up fine. She's rid of a philandering spendthrift husband. She's still young and attractive and most of all, wealthy. She should be able to start a wonderful new life for herself. What more could a girl ask for?"

"Do I sense a bit of sarcasm in that comment? After all you were part of the equation, weren't you?" I astounded myself how I could get right to the heart of an issue and not even feel uncomfortable. The truth spoken can be difficult to hear, but it always elicits a sense of freedom. That's what I was hoping for from Susan, an admission of truth. If not, I would have to bring in the big guns of eavesdropping evidence.

Susan didn't flinch. She stepped over her winch line and began rolling it symmetrically to match all the others. I noticed all her lines were laid out in this fashion. Nothing was out of place, not even Susan's own passions. Her tidiness wasn't a surprise to me because it seemed everything had its place in Susan's life.

"Listen, I don't know what you think you heard or saw or know, but my personal life is just that. Can I be more clear?" There was no rise or fall to the timbre of her voice. She simply adjusted her ball cap and headed below. She shuffled through a cupboard and brought up some teak oil to rub down the wood on the upper deck.

"I'm not asking about your personal life out of morbid curiosity," I replied when she returned. "This was attempted homicide, for Pete's sake."

"What does that have to do with me? It could have been anyone in the building that night who stuck the knife in his back. And it's a moot point anyhow. Are you trying to accuse me of something?"

I was finally getting some kind of a response, even if it was a bit more confrontational than I anticipated. "Should I be? You can't deny you were having a fling with him. I'm sorry, but it wasn't too difficult to overhear your heated conversation the night of the party."

Looking exasperated, Susan drew in a deep breath and slumped onto the cockpit cushion. "What are you looking for, an admission that Susan Fairfield was in an adulterous relationship? Yes, I was and now it's over, isn't it?" She turned in her seat, grabbed a cloth in a tightened fist and began rubbing the teak in a frenetic rhythm. Maybe she believed that the harder she rubbed the more she could lessen the guilt of an affair. Perhaps she was trying to scrub away the guilt of something more sinister.

For a moment I felt sorry for her. Here was a woman who appeared to have everything—looks, money, and career. But somehow, those things had not been enough. For her, life was all about image and prestige. I couldn't imagine being as independent as Susan Fairfield seemed to be, so distant from a real human relationship. On the other hand, maybe her detachment revealed how easily she could commit a crime as heinous as murder. My empathy died with Susan's quick tongue.

"I'd love to invite you in for cocktails, but as you can see, I've got work to do. So, if you don't mind." Without another word she shooed her unwanted company away with a brisk flip of her wrist.

I never took kindly to being dismissed, especially when I still had unanswered questions. I wanted to keep my feet firmly planted on the cockpit deck, but a hasty retreat would have to suffice. I jumped off the stern, turning with one last remark, the kind that gets people's tail feathers in a twist, the kind that makes the guilty think twice about their dirty deeds.

"Since you're a doctor I think you'll find this story of interest. When I was interning at the *Providence Journal*, I wrote a story about a man who used a lethal dose of arsenic to kill his wife. The doctors were stymied as to the cause of death. Certain poisons can be almost undetectable. He might have gotten away with it except for one small thing." I raised my finger and pointed, shaking it at Susan. "There's always just one forgotten thing and that's the one thing that gets the guilty person every time."

Susan glared. If she had been a dragon, smoke and fire would have billowed out of her ears. She never took her eyes off me until I reached the end of the dock. That was exactly the reaction I was hoping for because anger is the one emotion that can break a cold calculating heart.

If Susan were a murderer, then perhaps my taunt would cause her to slip up and leave the vital clue I needed.

CHAPTER 8

Monday, October 14

Thank goodness my store was closed on Mondays. Jessica, if available, would go tend to any animals we had in the store. This was great because the time off gave me a chance to run errands I couldn't do on Sundays, such as banking. Today I would add a little investigative reporting to my to-do list.

I rang the brass bell of the eighteen-thousand-square-foot home, wondering what I would see inside. A maid answered the door and let me into the foyer, then stepped out of the way of her stumbling employer. I could tell from the reek that Amanda Broward had started the lunch hour early with a few too many swills of scotch. With a mixture of pity and revulsion I studied the aging woman, wondering how life had taken so much from her that she needed alcohol to make it through the day.

I never met Frank's father, but wondered what he would think of such a woeful sight. This widow, who had remnants of a once attractive face, was now scarred by some hidden demons that were cruel not only to her, but also to those around her.

"You're here to see my little Frankie, aren't you? Well, come in. Would you like a drink?" She didn't wait for a response as she motioned for the maid and me to follow her. She teetered down the expansive marbled hall, its vaulted ceiling ascending a good twenty feet above our heads. We entered a small room to the right where one wall was covered with French doors made of leaded glass. The room overlooked a meticulously tended garden, still splendid in its form and color despite the season. "Have a seat at the bar, my dear."

I did as I was told as Amanda Broward ordered the maid in a discordant voice, "Ursula, go find Frankie and tell him to get in here and be quick about it."

The maid curtsied and replied with a quiet, "Yes ma 'am," and then left the room. I was astonished. I never imagined in today's me-oriented-politically-correct climate any person would curtsy except maybe to the Queen of England.

"May I offer you a wee dram of Scotch whisky, my dear?" she asked, as she slid onto the barstool next to mine. As with most of Mrs. Broward's questions, no answer was expected. Pointing to a tall black-labeled bottle she proudly began explaining the intricacies of a great single-malt whisky. "That is a bottle of 1974 Ardbeg scotch, which probably costs more than you make in a week. It's a single-malt whisky," she paused to express a hiccup. "In fact every bottle has its own unique characteristics. The local water and even proximity to the salty ocean air can make a subtle but discernable difference in its flavor."

She moved behind the bar and began lifting one bottle after another, pronouncing names I had never heard before. Finally she selected one, then poured the bronze-colored liquor into a short crystal tumbler filled with ice. She handed the drink to me. I sat bemused. "I know one should never shock a glass of good Scotch with ice, but I've never liked mine neat."

I wasn't sure how to respond. "Thanks," was the best I could muster and I lifted the glass, letting the cold liquid brush past my lips. When she turned away I poured the entire contents into a large potted plant on the bar. My reprieve came when Frank bounded into the room.

He gave his mother a disapproving glance, then quickly lifted my elbow and rushed me out the French doors to the stone patio beyond.

"I'm so *sowwy* I didn't get downstairs sooner. I hope my mother didn't make you too uncomfortable." Frank's embarrassment was notable. "She can *dwive* a person to a high-story window *wedge* and then make them feel like the fall is a joy *wide* compared to staying behind with her. I apologize; Susan must be *wubbing* off on me. What is it that you need?"

I gave Frank a comforting look. "She really knows a lot about Scotch whisky. I was actually rather impressed."

"It's in her blood. My maternal grandfather was Scottish born and *bwed.* Her maiden name was MacGregor. You can't get more Scottish than that. Besides her father owned quite a few *distillewys.* Anyway, how can I help you?"

"I was hoping you still had some leftover stuff so we could make another centerpiece."

"Why, did Carol and I forget to *dewiver* to one of the winners?"

"No, that's not it." I hoped my scathingly brilliant idea wouldn't seem too devious to a strait-laced guy like Frank. "It's just…I wanted to pop in and visit Mrs. Taglianno. She's a member and she attended the Fall Fest Ball." I waited for Frank to shake his head in recognition. "I thought delivering a centerpiece to one of the winners would be a good excuse to reintroduce myself."

Frank's confused and questioning look prompted a confession. I sat down on the wrought-iron bench flanking the patio and revealed my morbid motivation. "Okay, so she wasn't a winner. It's just I've got this unsettling feeling about Mr. Voorhees's death and something I overheard the evening of the party. I thought I might be able to clear some things up if I could get in to talk with her."

"Of course, the whole thing was unsettling," Frank, said. "He had a knife in his back. But the paper said he died from suspicious circumstances. This isn't good, but it didn't say murder. I know I shouldn't ask, but are you doing a *stowy* for the paper?" He sat down beside me and leaned into my shoulder.

"Do you remember the report a few years back about the guy who almost got away with poisoning his wife?" I asked. "Almost a year went by before the police came up with enough evidence to allow the family to exhume her body to do another autopsy. They eventually found traces of arsenic in her system that they traced back to her husband."

"Yes, I remember. She had a *warge wife* insurance policy and they decided it was the motive for murder. But what does that have to do with the Taglianno woman? You think she poisoned Voorhees?"

"Maybe not her. Maybe her husband, but there's no proof yet of anything," I hastened to add.

Frank looked at me skeptically.

"I know it sounds far-fetched," I said. "It's not like the days of Rasputin. It's just I can't seem to shake this feeling. I overheard a few conversations the night of the ball and they point to some prime suspects. I don't have proof, though, and that's why I want to go see Mrs. Taglianno."

"Are you certain you want to get involved? If you have information, why don't you take it to the *powice*? How about your friend, um, Lieutenant Sherman?"

"That's just it; I don't have any real information. Right now my suspicions are just part women's intuition and part common sense. Sherlock Holmes said, 'whenever you eliminate the impossible, whatever remains, however improbable, must be the truth.' Well, I'm trying to do just that, and I suspect the solution that's left may point to a murderer who attended the party."

"That makes sense. Someone did want to murder him. Why else the knife in his back, except the heinous deed came too late. What does Sherman think?"

"He says it is what it is until there's more evidence. I know he doesn't really believe the natural causes thing either, but his hands are tied. There's nothing anyone can do until the toxicology report comes back and that could be weeks. So, unless there's specific evidence, then death by suspicious heart attack is how it will stand unless they find out otherwise."

Frank shifted on the cold bench and stole a glance at his mother through the French doors. He stood, zipped his lip with his thumb and forefinger, locked his mouth and placed an imaginary key in his pocket. "I won't ask anything more. I've got every thing you'll need upstairs. It'll just take a minute. Wait here."

Most people don't like impromptu visits from virtual strangers. I hoped bearing gifts would soften the intrusion. I retrieved Taglianno's address from the computer files at the club and this time enlisted the help of the GPS system in the Volvo. With its annoying voice indicator, the device directed me over highways and rural roads until the diminutive voice announced, "Destination ahead."

I stopped in front of a well maintained, L-shaped cedar-shingled home. The house was far from ostentatious but appeared both charming and comfortable. I parked beside the road and walked up the drive feeling apprehensive. I hoped the infamous Grandpa Taglianno wasn't visiting today.

With a small box in one arm I pushed the doorbell with my free hand and waited, half-hoping no one would answer.

But soon the door swung open and a petite woman greeted me. She was rather like her house—simple, yet classic, in blue jeans and a light-pink cotton oxford shirt. Her jet-black hair was pulled back in a ponytail. A silver pendant dangled from a chain around her neck. The questioning look on her face prompted me to speak with conviction as I stretched out my hand in greeting. "Hello, Mrs. Taglianno, I'm Morgan Langdon from the yacht club. We met last weekend at the Fall Fest Ball. I hope I'm not intruding."

The momentary silence was deafening, but the woman's etiquette training must have kicked in, for she grabbed my hand in a firm shake. "Please call me Gina," she said and invited me into the living room. It was furnished with a plump, slip-cushioned couch and overstuffed chairs. I could have lived in that room with ease.

Before I sank into the cream colored upholstery, I laid my box on the floor and began pulling the items out one at a time and arranging them on the coffee table. The final piece was an oil lamp I placed in the center of the garland and ribbon wreath. "Tah dah," I announced. "We never had a chance at the ball to pull the winning tickets for the centerpieces, but you were one of the lucky recipients. Hope you like it."

With a sheepish smile Gina Taglianno caressed the ribbon and smiled, thanking me for taking time out of my busy schedule to hand deliver the prize. "This was so thoughtful of you to come all this way. Did you personally deliver to all the winners?"

"Oh no, the other committee members helped out. It's actually been rather an adventure tracking people down and surprising them." I was thinking more of Barbara Voorhees than anyone else.

"Still, it was very considerate of you." Standing, smoothing out her shirt and letting out a long breath, which I imagined was a precursor to a polite good-bye, she said, "May I offer you something to drink? I have soda, water, coffee, or…I just went over to Connecticut the other day and brought back some apple cider. Would you like some?"

"That would be perfect. Thank you." I watched her glide out of the room. The kitchen must have been on the other side of the wall because I could hear her humming and the refrigerator being opened and closed. She came back in with cookies and some crackers that had some sort of homemade concoction spread on top. To wash it down were two tall glasses of freshly pressed cider. This was far better tasting than the other caramel-colored drink I'd had earlier.

"Did you get this cider at McIntosh Farm on the other side of Route One?"

"Yes. I love that place, especially this time of year." Gina sipped her drink and for a moment the polite conversation, finger foods, and sublime layout of the room made me imagine I was in Martha Stewart's house.

I wondered how a woman so provincial managed to marry a man so unconventional, but maybe those Mafia stereotypes of husband and wife relationships are just as far-fetched as they seem. This woman was demure and soft-spoken. She seemed to be the perfect wife. I took a bite of a cracker. "I'd love to get the recipe for whatever this is on top. It's delicious," I said.

Gina blushed and said, "It's a simple vegetarian pâté: artichoke hearts, walnuts, fresh rosemary, and basil. The secret lies in fresh ingredients. I grow my own herbs and vegetables in the greenhouse in the backyard. That's really the trick, chopping everything fresh. I'll write down the recipe for you before you leave."

"Thanks. That would be great," I replied, shoving down an entire cracker in one bite. Conversation ebbed for a moment while I chewed, swallowed and pictured my mother-in-law trying this tasty tidbit made with my own little hands. After I wiped my mouth, the dialogue continued.

"I'm curious. May I ask what other members won a centerpiece?" Gina asked.

"Of course. It's no big secret." But I realized in part it *was* a secret because Gina's winning was only a figment of my fertile imagination. "There were about sixteen winners." I rattled off as many names as I could remember. Then for an extra punch I saved Barbara Voorhees's name for last. "One of the winners, sadly, was Mrs. Voorhees. In fact I went to visit her just yesterday. She seems to be doing well for a woman who recently lost her husband, and under such questionable circumstances."

"I'm sorry. I don't know what you mean. I assumed from the paper and the rumors it was health issues."

"For now they're saying that. Actually the police are still investigating the specifics."

"I see," was her only response.

Since that tack wasn't working I tried another. "Do you know the Voorheeses very well?" I cast my line and waited to reel in a big one.

"Not well. I knew they had been members for a short while. I do know about Mr. Voorhees's jewelry stores. My husband and I have been to the one in Boston." She sighed, adding, "My husband is more interested in the more glitzy, what do they say today, bling-bling? Although we do have a few heirloom pieces I am quite fond of."

"I'm the same way. I love looking at the big carat stuff, but most of it I would never be caught dead in." My words were an inappropriate slip of the tongue. I hoped Gina wouldn't collapse from the sheer tactlessness of my remark, but I saw I had hit a chord when she responded with a sly smile.

I rushed on. "I guess I assumed your husband was more familiar with Mr. Voorhees than you since I saw them talking on the back deck at the party last weekend." Playing bashful I added, "They must have been talking business. You know how men can be. You try to dress them up for a nice evening, but it always turns to business or sports. With my husband it's always golf."

"I know what you mean. Tony was off talking most of the evening about his computers and all the new programs and gadgets. Trying to drum up business, I'm sure. In fact, that's probably the conversation you saw him in with Mr. Voorhees." Gina turned away, standing to pick up the food plate. "If I'm remembering correctly, Emile Voorhees was purchasing an accounting program and new computers from us. Yes, I'm sure that's what you overheard."

She retreated into the kitchen. As I watched her go, I had to wonder if she was trying to convince me that the conversation was innocent or was she trying to convince herself? Within a moment she returned with another plate, this one piled high with warm gingersnaps.

I said, "New technology fascinates me, but I really don't understand how any of it works. I'm lucky I can manage my cash register and GPS system." I crunched on a bite of cookie, allowing time for the next question to form in my sugar-laden brain. "How did your husband become interested in that type of business? Has he always been into computers?"

I could see the wheels of prudence turning. "He took computer science in college. Then he worked for his father for a short period of time, helping to manage the family's many businesses. His dad had never jumped into the twenty-first century to keep track of inventory and payroll and whatnot, so Tony devised a system for networking all the business's computers. Once he managed that, he designed an accounting and inventory program. His system worked so well that he decided to go into business for himself. His father discouraged him, but Tony is very strong-willed."

I saw from the shifting of Gina's weight on the couch that this was an uncomfortable conversation and I wondered what expectations a father might have for his son. Thinking better of asking that specific question, I wondered how a man might go about telling his Mafia father that he no longer wants to be in the family business.

"I'm sure," I said and gulped down a mouthful of cider, knowing Gina would never divulge the truth about her father-in-law. Eating my sixth cookie I pondered the possibility that her husband might actually have gone legitimate, leaving behind so much influence and money to become his own boss and work fifty-hour weeks. I found such a move almost too hard to believe, but I hoped it had happened, if only for Gina Taglianno's sake.

Not wanting to overstay my welcome, I wiped my mouth clean. "Maybe we'll see you down at the club. We own *Irish Eyes.* She's used but in good condition. How about you, are you slipped or moored?"

"We own *Dolce Vendetta*. She's docked. We don't get out as much as we'd like to. Work and volunteering activities keep us pretty busy. Sometimes I like to get away and go down and just sit on the boat. Do you ever do that?" She asked, as if looking for affirmation.

"All the time. Just sitting and enjoying the rocking motion and the sounds of the halyard snapping against the mast…life doesn't get much better than that—except with a bottle of good wine," I said.

She smiled as I thanked her for the recipe and letting me barge in unannounced. I threw on my jacket and left wiping my brow, thankful no other Tagliannos had arrived while I was there. It wasn't that I believed all the stories I'd heard about this infamous family, but Nick's cautiousness was rubbing off on me. If Taglianno were a murderer, then who was to stop him from killing again, especially if he felt threatened by a short, meddlesome, size-six blonde.

CHAPTER 9

Tuesday, October 15

Tuesday was the first day of the business week at Paws For Love. Sundays and Mondays the store was closed to customers, but not always to work. Thank goodness for part-time help.

I enjoyed having a weekday off to get things done, but I'd spent Monday playing detective, so I'd pushed some of the household duties over to Tuesday. Today I was stuck in the shop on my own because Jessica had classes all day. Her absence was actually a blessing, for it meant a little welcome solitude and fewer cash register mistakes. The fewer mistakes there were the easier it was for me at the end of the day when I had to balance the books.

Shipments of food, toys and pet paraphernalia arrived weekly. Their delivery meant plenty of backbreaking lifting and shuffling. My first task every morning was to clean, feed and give lots of loving to whatever small pets I had in the store at the time. Care of animals is paramount in my business and in pet ownership, too. I am always careful to screen potential buyers and I make purchasers watch a DVD on what to expect and how to care for their new pet. Impulsiveness and purchasing a pet are never a good combination.

This week my store was home to two female Dumbo ear rats and a ferret. On slow days playing with the animals is the best part of my job. Today, I was exceptionally attentive to the rats because I believe they got an unfair bad reputation during the Black Plague. In reality the fleas carried the disease; the rats were just a convenient form of transportation.

I was in the back room towel drying the ferret after its bath when the bell jangled on my front door. I plopped the animal down inside her temporary housing, being sure to close the latch. Ferrets are experts at escaping through the narrowest of openings. Peering out the storeroom door, I was stunned to see Mrs. Broward with her son, Frank, for the second day in a row. I bypassed the idea of taking off my apron and combing my hair. Instead I made a beeline toward my visitors.

"Hello. This is an unexpected surprise. What can I do for you?" I smiled at Mrs. Broward but took a backward questioning glance at Frank who looked like an overwrought Tasmanian devil. His thumbs were circling each other in double-time as he swayed back and forth on his heels. I could tell this wasn't a friendly drop-in.

"Mother, why don't you *wook awound*? I need to talk to Morgan for a moment." Frank whisked me to the back room where he apologized repeatedly for disturbing me and guaranteed that he and his mother wouldn't stay long.

"Stop apologizing. Your mother's not disturbing me, but you are. Why are you so wound up, Frank? I mean your mom actually seems sober for a change."

Frank looked down at his loafers and chewed on the inside of his cheek.

I continued, "I know you don't have a pet and I'm certain you don't want to purchase a rat, so why are you here with that guilty look on your face?"

"If you think my mother's a force when's she tipsy you should see her when she's sober. She insisted that I tell her why you stopped by the other day." Noticing the wide-eyed glare from me he said, "No, no, don't *wowwy*. I didn't say a thing. The *pwobwem* is now she thinks you were there to *bowwow* money and I can't seem to dissuade her otherwise. She insisted on coming down and checking out your store and asking you about your finances." He sat down, placed his face in his hands and shook his head. "I am so *sowwy*. If I were only more…more…anything!" He paused, slapping his hand on his hound's-tooth wool pants. "More *bwave*, more authoritative, more assertive, then maybe she wouldn't walk all over me, maybe no one would."

I was at a loss for words. I wanted to say some magic words to produce the man Frank wanted to be, but a shoulder hug was all I could muster.

"Let's go out and talk to your mother. We both know why I was there, and if it comes down to it, I'll just tell her the truth. No big deal."

"No big deal. Oh, you don't know my mother. Far better she *bewieves* you wanted to *bowwow* a boatload of cash than to know you were involving me in some kind of conspiracy theory. She could *dwink* like a fish in front of her *fwiends*, but never let anyone think she or her son is involved in something scandalous. She shuns tabloid stories and is paranoid about somebody finding a skeleton in the family closet."

"Conspiracy-schmearacy! She's a walking distillery, that's what she should worry about. For pity sakes, this doesn't have anything to do with her or you. It's me. Besides, does she really think she's so important that the *National Enquirer* would want to do a scoop on her? Forgive me, Frank, but your mother is loopier than I thought."

"Do me this one favor. Just tell her you came for advice on party themes for the next yacht *cwub* gathering."

Frank's face so resembled a lost dog I couldn't refuse him. "All right, all right. Whatever you say." The wrinkles in my brow were sure to set like stone years before menopause if I had to deal with Mrs. Broward much longer. I didn't mind for myself as much as I couldn't stand the effect she had on Frank. I wished I had known his father. Maybe Frank's male parent was the reason someone so thoughtful and sensitive had sprung from the loins of Medusa's sister. Taking a deep breath, I stepped out from the back room and confronted her.

"Mrs. Broward, Frank says you're concerned about my visit yesterday, and I want to assure you that I am totally innocent of any panhandling. All I needed was his creative expertise." Thinking on my feet, I said, "The yacht club will be planning holiday festivities for December and I just wanted to pick his brain for ideas." Seeing her skepticism, I moved in closer and looked straight at her drooping, over-made-up eyelids. "Your son is very talented. He did a wonderful job helping with the Fall Fest Ball."

"You don't need to explain my son to me. As for the Ball, well…" she paused for effect, "if he were as good as you say then we would never have been held prisoners by a storm and a death. As for his money, it's safe in an account with both our names on it. So don't think I won't know if you try anything." She patted her purse with confidence. "Frank, we need to get going. I have a bridge game waiting for me. Come along."

Frank looked up from the floor. What more could he say? After all, his mother was the reigning matriarch. He waved his thanks in my direction, helped his mother down the five concrete steps that descended from my shop to the street and tucked her into the waiting Bentley.

I was left standing inside, mouth agape, stomping my feet. "Could anyone be more exasperating than that woman?" I said out loud to the only living thing in the shop that could understand me, Cooper. "I swear one of these days I'm going to email Doctor Phil and ask him how to force a self-righteous, rigid unfeeling woman to acquire just one admirable personality trait." I paused, crouched to Cooper's level, and kissed him on the nose. "Impossible, I know. Let's get back to work."

A few hours later Nick stopped by with a pizza for lunch. It was a ritual. He allowed himself an hour and fifteen minutes for lunch every Tuesday. It gave us a little quality time together before the start of the usually busy week. We were enjoying our white basil and sun-dried tomato pizza when another familiar face appeared at my door.

"This must be the day for yacht club members," I said out loud. As soon as the words were out of my mouth and I saw the look on Nick's face, I realized I had trapped myself. If I told Nick about the Browards stopping in, I would have to explain my earlier visit to their house. The one thing I can never do and get away is lying to Nick. He knows me too well. How could I explain taking a raffle wreath to a non-winner, especially when that person was a Taglianno? But it was too late because standing by the shelf filled with squeaky toys was Tony Taglianno himself.

With knees shaking and palms sweating, I smiled a hearty smile. "Hello. May I help you?"

There was no polite gesture, no how-do-you-do. Just simply, "You can help me by staying away from my wife. She may be naïve about meddling, but I'm not. You're prying into things that aren't your business, so leave well enough alone before you have regrets." He left no time for a comeback as he turned to exit, leaving the door open behind him.

"What was that all about?" Nick asked. He turned his Superman x-ray vision glare on me. I could see he was asking for a straight answer without a lot of twaddle.

I had never been happier with my dog clock for at that precise moment it barked two, the end of the lunch hour. "Look at the time. You've got to get back to Mrs. Ornsby and her root canal. You know how persnickety she can be when she's kept waiting. I'll tell you all about it later this evening after I run a few errands. You're on your own for dinner. Love you. See ya." As the words were rolling off my tongue I rushed him and the leftover pizza out to his car. He tried bellowing his frustration, but in the end had to settle for a worried glance over the steering wheel in place of explanations.

Wiping the imagined sweat from my brow, I contemplated the series of tales I could spin to get myself off the hook, but this time nothing came to me. I chalked my mental lapse up to fear, but fear couldn't stop my mission. Stubbornness is one of my finer qualities. After work I went to the local superstore and bought myself a large hat and glasses. The disguise, along with a Southern drawl, would have to suffice when I visited Voorhees's Newport store later on that afternoon.

Tuesday 5:20 P. M.

I hurriedly closed the store a bit after five leaving the paperwork for morning. I drove over the bridge leading across Narragansett Bay and arrived at Beauty by Design just before closing.

A woman wearing a well-tailored suit dress met me. She uttered a polite if not stuffy, "Good afternoon. May we design something for you or is there a particular piece you are looking for?"

In my best genteel inflection I mused, "My husband's interested in purchasing me an anniversary gift, but I thought it best to look first. Do you mind?" I imagined a large mint julep in my hand as I was escorted to a plush rolling chair facing a glass case full of gems. My heart beat wildly. If only I really were here to search for an anniversary gift, but Nick's idea of romance was two tickets to a Red Sox game and a couple of hotdogs, not a two-carat sapphire laced with diamond baguettes.

"What may I show you?" The woman retrieved a diamond and sapphire teardrop necklace from the display case.

"Let me try this one on you. It's one of our more popular pieces and runs a mere forty-two hundred dollars."

I felt like hot butter melting off the chair. She said forty-two hundred dollars as if people spent that kind of money at the drop of a hat every day in her store. Who knows? Maybe they do, but I don't. I remembered the day last Christmas when I bought myself a tennis bracelet at the local department store for four hundred dollars and thought it was a big investment.

I had to stay in character, though, so I replied with, "It's lovely, but a bit too ostentatious for my taste. Let's try looking at some bracelets instead." As the woman began pulling out satin-covered boards for presentation, I started reeling her in. I was working on the presumption this woman was like all employees: she talked about the boss behind his back and shared what she knew with others.

"I was so sad to hear about Mr. Voorhees's death. It must have been quite a blow to the employees," I said.

"Yes, it was quite a shock." Then, lifting a piece into her palm, she said, "How about this one?"

I shook my head no. "His wife must be devastated, poor thing. To lose a husband at such a young age or so I read in the paper."

"We never really see much of Mrs. Voorhees. Everything is managed by Emile and Richard Taylor, his partner." Excusing her personal reference she rephrased and said, "I meant, Mr. Voorhees."

Wondering if this was another one of Voorhees's admiring mistresses, I continued. "Well, it's a good thing they never had children. How awful for a mother to have to raise her children alone. Lucky her, though, I'm sure she'll inherit all of the businesses."

"Inherit? I'm not sure how all that works. I do know she owned at least half of the businesses herself. Mr. Voorhees and Mr. Taylor co-owned and managed them." Then deliberately under her breath she whispered, "He really managed to run them into the ground."

"I'm sorry. I didn't catch that."

Blushing she grabbed another piece, holding it close to my face. "How could you not love this one? Look how those pink diamonds sparkle."

I looked around at a store devoid of customers. "Oh, I see what you mean. Men can be so fickle. My husband could spend all his money on sports and betting and alcohol if I didn't rope him in." I hoped my list was long enough for Emile's bad behavior to fall into one of those categories.

I must have hit a nerve, because the perfectly powdered face behind the counter leaned closer and murmured, "I've worked for Beauty by Design for ten years and I could tell you things that would curl your toes."

I leaned into the counter knowing I was in for quite a ride.

6:15 P.M.

I held the door and turned the knob with a gentle grip, hoping not to a make a noise. The problem was Cooper. He could hear a mouse crawl across the carpeted floor with the television at full blast. I imagined the back-door latch sounded like the Fourth of July to him. There must have been some truth in my perception because he came bounding into the kitchen, barking his enthusiasm upon seeing me. Nick followed a few feet behind him with a tight grin and arms crossed.

"Well, my Irish Eyes, where have you been this evening?"

"Running those errands I mentioned to you earlier?"

"Yes, you also mentioned you would explain what Mr. Taglianno meant this afternoon when he left so, shall I say, abruptly."

"I did, didn't I? Goodness, some people can be so sensitive. I only…" My words trailed off.

"Stop, please. Whatever you did, whatever you're involved in now may have been altruistic in the fight for truth and justice, but your motives are pure and simple. You want the scoop no matter what the cost, even if the cost is a pair of cement pumps."

"That's not true. I'm always after the truth, nothing else. Listen to what I found out this evening and then tell me I haven't got a great story."

We sat at the kitchen table, Cooper at our feet, ears perked. "Talk about a treasure chest of information given to me this evening. There are possible, even conceivable, notions that Barbara Voorhees or drug dealers or even an angry partner may have wanted Emile disposed of."

I began by explaining how fortuitous I had been in speaking to the right person at Voorhees's store. The sales clerk either had major employee angst or didn't care what she revealed because dead men can't talk. The information she divulged may have been guesswork, but the motives were as clear-cut as a rainforest in Brazil. The woman's diatribe against Mr. and Mrs. Voorhees provided enough material for a Monday night movie. Most of the information was speculative at best, but at least it gave me a direction to follow. It seems Voorhees had many affairs before Susan, and if that wasn't enough to rock the marital boat, he flaunted his liaisons to anyone who cared. He took his girlfriends to the Indian Casino in Connecticut on a regular basis and he lavished them with gifts and cash to gamble. He told his wife he was schmoozing the casino brass into allowing him to open a retail store. His excuses must have begun to ring hollow to Barbara as they would to me if I were in her shoes.

Then there was Richard Taylor, the partner who owned twenty-four percent of the shares in the company. He was adept at managing a retail business, but was totally clueless about the quality of the gems themselves. Rumor had it that Emile was substituting the real thing with excellent fakes and so far no customer had noticed the difference. According to his employee, he sold the real diamonds on the black market and used the proceeds to pay off his gambling and drug debts. Was it possible Taylor heard these rumors and found them to be true? Perhaps Emile was using smoke and mirrors to hide the fact that the business was sinking into bankruptcy. Worse, maybe the drug dealers themselves weren't happy with an addict who was overdrawn from the drug bank.

I believed these were all strong motives for any number of people to have committed murder. Even Nick, who wasn't sure what to think and wasn't happy I was doing so much investigative footwork on my own, still felt compelled enough to believe some of the gossip might be true. But staying one step ahead of a killer and separating fact from fiction might be a trick even Cooper couldn't handle.

CHAPTER 10

Friday, October 18

"Honey, have you seen my blue sweater with the yellow stripes? I can't seem to find it anywhere." Nick was rummaging through the hangers in the closet when I rounded the corner in our bedroom.

"I already packed it. You better get going or you're going to miss your plane."

Nick didn't enjoy most dental seminars, especially when golfing wasn't in the curriculum. This weekend would be no exception. It was Friday and he was headed for New York City out of Providence for a two-day lecture on laser dentistry. I had to stay behind at Paws for Love. Jessica was having midterms and, although she could come across as ditsy and scattered-brained on occasion, her grades were a serious subject.

"Don't forget your cell phone. I've got your briefcase if you want to grab your carry-on."

The screen door banged behind us as we raced to the car. I leaned in, throwing Nick's briefcase onto the passenger seat. Nick tossed his luggage into the trunk and gave me a soft kiss good-bye, promising he would phone when he got to the hotel.

"Say bye to Cooper for me. Tell him we'll go for a long walk on the beach when I get back on Sunday. And you, young lady, promise me you won't follow any more fact-finding hunches until you talk to your editor and me!" He closed the door and with a stern look mouthed I love you as he drove down the driveway and out of sight.

I smiled and blew him a kiss with my right hand, but I crossed my fingers behind my back with the other. I had every intention of talking to my editor, but not until I had more facts.

The workday passed by at its usual tempo. Nick called and checked in once he arrived at the convention hotel. After we hung up I organized the chew toys and squeaky balls, stocked the shelves with extra cat and dog treats, checked the inventory and placed a few orders. I dealt with customers and did the chore that was the least fun, paying bills. In between all the shuffling, I had time to reflect on the events of the past two weeks. I had checked with Mark Sherman on the tox report. It detected some type of offending substance, which caused it to be sent back through for more analysis. We were now looking at another week or two and still no one being charged. The police were at a standstill when it came to who had used the knife. I was becoming more convinced of foul play. My intuition, along with a few facts, was beginning to scream like a banshee in distress. I wanted to be careful, however, I remembered Hercule Poirot exhorting something like: *one shouldn't distort the facts just to support a theory.*

With the wealth of information I had obtained from the Newport employee, I could only imagine the possibilities if I went to the Boston stores. I was going over the logistics in my head as I spoke out loud and paced around the shelving. "If I leave for Boston tomorrow morning, I could be there when the stores open. That should give me plenty of time to stop at the store in Brockton first. Then I'll make my way up to Boston and Nick never need know, at least not now. Of course, I'll have to cancel our nursing home visit."

Cooper, who had far better sense than I, cocked his head and moaned like a bear. It was his way of acknowledging my pacing and thinking out loud. I did both a lot, even at home. Walking and talking helped my mind work faster when trying to solve a problem. Like the time when we had two weddings at two, an after-hour's tooth extraction, and a dinner party all scheduled on the same day. Communication was never one of Nick's strong suits. Managing our personal lives was always left up to me. That day I had worn a path around the hall through the living room and back again talking to myself until I finally solved the problem. The tooth extraction was rescheduled for late morning. Then we went to one church for the first two o'clock wedding, skipped the first reception so we could make it to the second reception, then left by five to make the dinner party. Exhausting, but it worked.

Organization was my strong point so I was certain I would be able to pack in all the traveling and interrogation I needed before Nick returned home.

Saturday, October 19

I champed at the bit all Friday afternoon and evening. Saturday morning, after a long brisk walk with Cooper, I apologized to him for not being able to take him in the car with me.

The drive to Brockton took a little over an hour. I had come prepared again with thick-rimmed glasses and a hat, in part to elude embarrassment. If this whole thing turned out to be a simple coronary, I didn't want to be remembered as an interfering busybody if someday I actually did decide to purchase myself a nice cocktail ring. On the other hand, if the death really had been murder, I didn't want the murderer recognizing me for fear of reprisal.

My GPS saved me again as I pulled into the parking lot of the second store Voorhees opened four years after his Boston store became such a success. His slogan on billboards was, "Let Us Design It for the Beauty within You." The motto was written in black and gold and was often accompanied by a photo of a beautiful child held by a captivating woman and a chiseled-cheeked man who all wore original designs by Emile. The images made you want to buy from Beauty by Design so you could be as striking as the people in the portrait.

I walked into the store with my nose as high as I could muster without tripping in my three-inch heels.

"Good afternoon. May we design something for you or are you looking for a particular piece?"

I felt a sense of déjà vu as the attractive woman approached me. Her red hair pulled back in a tight bun, her figure clad in a gray tailored suit, and her scarlet-painted fingernails outstretched.

"Is this the store that promises to design a piece of jewelry with my beauty in mind because I'm interested in an anniversary gift for myself."

"Of course." The employee smirked as if she saw right through my haughty disguise. Without flinching, though, she led me to a few paisley-covered chairs in the far corner of the room. "Have a seat and let me show you our newest design. Then we can go from there." Just as before the employee began pulling out satin-covered boards to display the glittering gems. And just as before I began my not-so-subtle cross-examination.

"New designs, you said? That surprises me. Wasn't the owner, oh what was his name now…Mr. Vullhees, no no, Nolmeers, oh whatever…didn't I read he died?"

Her face flushed as she answered in a condescending, corrective voice. "Voorhees. His name is, excuse me, I mean *was*, Mr. Emile Voorhees. These particular designs I am speaking of were some of the last designs he created just a little over a month ago. The Boston store and ours are the only ones to carry these pieces. We just released them to the public this week. They are sure to go up in value." She lifted a platinum and gold bangle from the case below and laid it on a purple satin board. The design reminded me of a Celtic knot. The raised engraving circled around the circumference of the bangle, its line interrupted every three knots by a rectangular quarter-carat emerald. "This particular piece is twelve hundred dollars," the woman said.

For a moment I forgot myself and wondered how much money we had in our checking account. My Irish was demanding I purchase this fairly priced bangle as a Christmas gift for me from Nick. How perfect would it be to wake up Christmas morning and find this bracelet dangling from a satin ribbon on the tree? If I truly was Nick's only Irish-lass then he shouldn't mind.

My stupefied gaze didn't go unnoticed. "I'd be glad to wrap it up for you today. Will this be charge or cash?"

"Oh, no thank you. I would want my husband to see it first. I'm just here to do some preliminary shopping." I gave a polite smile as I tried to lap up the imaginary drool hanging from my lip. The employee stifled a chuckle as she leaned into the display case to gather a few more items. As she did so, I noticed a necklace dangling over her generous bosom. As it swayed back and forth, it sparkled in the light. I reached out and lifted it away from her neck. It was a silver heart set with a marquis diamond in the middle. "Isn't that pretty. Is it an original?"

Blushing crimson she stood and tucked the necklace inside the collar of her silk blouse. "No, this is a one-of-a-kind design. Mr. Voorhees creates one for every employee who stays with the company for a year. The women get a necklace and the men receive a tie clasp." Rubbing the necklace through her blouse, she added, "Of course, now that he's gone, I'm not sure what the tradition will be. Would you like to see some earrings? If you liked the design of the bangle, we have matching earrings and rings."

I gave a sure-go-ahead shake of my head as the faithful employee went around to another case to locate the items. I wondered if all Voorhees's workers were as sentimental and coy about their personal gifts. Perhaps the pieces were meant as keep-your-nose-out-of-my-business rewards. If employees looked the other way when questionable practices arose, then they received nice things in payment. Or, more than likely, the gifts were meant as *quid pro quo:* you give me what I want and you'll get what you want.

The employee presented a few more enticing items. I began wishing I really were here to purchase, not pilfer information. I lifted the jewelry pieces one at a time, making cooing sounds over each one. Then, just as an expert gemologist shapes a gem, I crafted my question. "What will become of these lovely stores? I've heard rumors that his partner doesn't really know much about the jewelry business, let alone design."

"Rumors are just that. Mr. Taylor, Voorhees's partner, plans to hire new designers. In fact he's already in the process of making some changes to the company." Correcting what could have been seen as a crass comment, she added, "Of course he's very saddened by the death of his partner, as most all of us are."

I took note of the adjective *most* and wondered if the sadness included her. "Oh, I'm sure you're right," I said, "but you know how rumors can be. They start out innocent enough. Then they slide down that slippery slope of gossip and falsities begin to ring true. For instance, I'm from Newport where he owns another store, and I heard from the locals that Voorhees was running his business into the ground with his drugs and gambling." Then appealing to her empathetic side, I said,

"Can you believe what some people will say once a person is dead?"

"Rumors always fly when people are powerful and successful," Ms. Perfect Employee said, rubbing the back of her neck. I wondered if there might be more truth than fiction in the tales. I could see this employee wasn't going to be as cooperative as the last one, for she began dismantling the jewelry stands in mid-sentence. Then, in a tone that implied she was finished showing jewelry, she asked, "Are there any last items I can show you?"

Not knowing where I could take the conversation, I acquiesced. "No. I suppose not. I'll have to bring my husband in later next week. Thank you for your time. You were very helpful."

I left not knowing any more than I had known earlier. The one thing that changed, though, was that tingling sensation down my spine. It had now become a full-fledged shiver that I hoped a visit to the Boston store might squelch.

I drove another forty-five minutes before I got through the traffic and found my way to a street off Boston Common. I had to park a few blocks away from Beauty by Design because Saturday shoppers had taken all the prime parking spots. Christmas patrons started earlier every year it seemed to me as I wound my way through the crowd of people with their bulky purchases hanging from their arms.

The shop was located in an old brownstone with large cedar doors. Bay windows lined with black velvet flanked the entrance, forming the perfect backdrop for the latest haute couture designs in jewelry. Even if a passerby didn't know the difference between a baguette and pavé, what was the difference? Every piece sparkled like the aurora borealis on a cold winter night and lured impulse buyers into the store.

I moved out of the way as a couple with a small gold bag left the shop arm-in-arm. They made me miss Nick and wish he were with me. For a moment I wondered what I was thinking coming here alone to search for some obscure clue to a murder no one believed had even been committed.

The Boston store was the largest store of the three and the site where most of the designing was done. Gray and burgundy paisley covered the furniture and gold plush carpet cushioned my feet. The display cases were a bit worn on the edges from ten years of customers leaning against them, but overall the feeling was one of opulence. As before, an employee, this time a man in a black pinstriped suit, greeted me with the all too familiar, "Good afternoon. May we design something for you or are you looking for a particular piece?"

I wanted to ask him if he ever felt like a Star Wars robot with the dress code and programmed greeting but decided against it. "I'm just going to browse if you don't mind."

"That would be fine. I'm with another customer for the moment, but I'll be with you as soon as I can."

My bladder was feeling the effects of the large coffee I had purchased earlier in the morning. "Do you have a ladies' room I could use?" I asked as the salesman quickly turned away from me.

"Through that opening between the back two displays, down the hall and make a right."

"Thanks." I followed his directions. The back rooms were quiet. I concluded that everyone else must have been out front or in some other area of the building because once I rounded the corner I couldn't hear any voices. Brass plates on each closed door identified what lay behind. One said OFFICE SUPPLIES, another NEIL KING ACCOUNTANT, and the last one before the ladies' room, EMILE VOORHEES. I shot a look over my shoulder before ducking inside the room and closing the door behind me. My bladder would have to wait.

The room was eerily quiet. I flipped on a light, as the room had no windows. To the right stood a credenza that housed a professional-looking coffee and espresso maker, its stainless steal polished to perfection. I felt strange as I imagined Voorhees sitting behind the massive, cherry wood desk nestled near the back wall. Walking over to it I touched the leather chair he would have sat in as he trudged through the requirements of his workday. I wondered what secrets he might have kept out of the view of curious eyes. A few design sketches he had made on a notepad lay next to his phone. I thought it must be true that inspiration can strike at odd times. On the other end of his desk perched a silver-framed picture of himself and his wife in some tropical setting and another of them on their sailboat passing by the Beavertail Light House in Fisher's Island Sound. I was sure of the setting because Nick and I had sailed by the lighthouse on *Irish Eyes* many times ourselves. What I found most intriguing, though, was that his desk calendar lay open to Wednesday, October 2. Three days before he died.

As I leaned in to get a closer look, I heard voices in the hall. Moving fast, I pulled the executive chair away from the desk far enough to slide my small frame into the kneehole. I held my breath, not making a sound but fearing my pounding heart might give me away. It was beating as loud as a tribal drum and I was sure anyone within whispering distance could hear it.

My worst fear came true as the door opened and in walked a person whose voice was not that of the helpful salesman out front. The stranger closed the door behind him and began talking to himself. His padding footsteps and the smell of his cologne gave me a sickening feeling when he moved, positioning himself right in front of the desk.

I tensed, awaiting inevitable discovery.

CHAPTER 11

"Where would you have put those invoices, Emile?" The man's frustration was evident in the way he shuffled through the desk papers, file cabinets and credenza, ripping out files and spilling their contents. "You screwed me while you were alive you smarmy liar. I'm not about to let you do it from your grave." The man leaned over Emile's desk and flipped the calendar around to face him. "What secrets do you still have hidden from me?" His tone was fraught with anger.

"Mr. Taylor? We need you out front." A muffled voice sounded from the hallway.

Richard Taylor jumped in his shoes, straightened his jacket, took a few long strides and opened the door. He called back, "I was just looking for some paperwork Emile and I went over last month." He gave an aggravated sigh and then closed the door behind him.

Divine providence was on my side. I wasn't sure what excuse could have gotten me out of this fix. Thankfully, I wouldn't have to find out. I crawled out from my hideaway, taking a deep breath while I stretched my legs and wondered what Taylor had been looking for. My eyes fell upon Emile's eighteen-month desktop calendar opened to the week of his death. I couldn't help thinking a person's calendar mirrors their true inner self.

Nick's and my refrigerator calendar reads pretty much the same from week to week, depending on the season. Wednesday is always golf league. Fridays and Saturdays are exclusively our date nights. Saturday afternoon is typically a nursing home visit for Cooper and me. Emile's calendar didn't scream such domestic simplicity.

I flipped through the pages seeing dinner dates at casinos and after-hours meetings at fancy restaurants, but nowhere did I see Barbara's name. The omission seemed sad to me. I relish time with my husband.

I wondered how on earth I was going to remember all the names and dates. I couldn't take the calendar. Someone would notice for certain and in addition I could be put in jail for stealing.

I propped my elbows on the desk, getting a closer look while contemplating my memory deficit. As I bent, my purse slid from my shoulder and fell to the floor, spilling its contents. Exasperated I bent to shovel things back inside and spotted my cell phone. Inspiration struck. I loved technology and here was a technological solution to my problem. My cell phone can take pictures and send them to my email address. Granted, the only photos I had taken thus far were of Cooper and Nick on the golf course, but this was the answer to my can't-remember-a-name-or-date-to-save-my-life problem.

I needed to act in haste. Any moment could bring another unwelcome visitor to the office and that was the last thing I wanted or needed. I turned on the desk lamp and flipped through the pages to twelve months previous. A years' activity should pretty much sum up a person's life, I assumed. When the book was open flat it showed one complete week, Sunday to Sunday. I clicked as quickly as I could, taking a shot of every other week, hoping something significant would appear when I examined them later. When I finished, I turned the pages back to the week before Voorhees died, flipped off the light switch and tiptoed toward the door. Opening it a crack, I peeped out to see if the hallway was clear. It was, so I slipped into the hall and closed the office door behind me. My bladder was now as backed up as the Hoover Dam, so I raced for the toilet at the end of the hall.

I received a queer look from the employee who had pointed the way to the restroom twenty minutes earlier. I smiled at him and left the building. I didn't think talking with anyone at this point could prove as profitable as the information I might get from Emile's calendar. Besides I was eager to get my pictures sent to my computer before I could accidentally erase them. I remembered the time I had entered over one hundred names into a mail merge, planning to send out sales flyers to my customers. With one click of the mouse, I managed to erase every one of them.

Sitting in my car where I had parked less than an hour earlier, I brought each picture up onto the screen, punched in our email address and pushed "send." This method took me far longer than I expected, for my stomach was announcing dinnertime. I began debating what to do for dinner, fast food drive-through or fast food eat-in, either way; fast food seemed the answer until a name flashed into my head. One of Voorhees's favorite places I had noticed while skimming through his calendar was Finnigan's Bar & Grill. On went the GPS, up came restaurants, in went the letters spelling Finnigan, and up came the map. I turned the ignition and started driving.

It was dark by the time I pulled into Finnigan's parking area near the Charles River. I wondered how safe a small, nosy blonde would feel eating alone in a place like this, but the restaurant looked harmless enough, at least from the outside. The building was in good shape, with its brick facing and clapboard sides clean and in good repair. I wondered if this was a new building meant to look old or the other way around.

Above the doorway hung a ship's wheel and a carved sign that read "Finnigan's" in large green letters. Inside, authentic Irish music played and electrified ships' lanterns hung from the post-and-beam construction. The lighting was dim. At the far end of the room stood a long bar with a brass footrest that ran the length of back wall. I decided the end of the oak bar would be a good place to grab an appetizer and perhaps some informative conversation.

"How many for dinner?" The hostess asked.

"Just one. May I sit at the bar and eat?"

"Sure, no problem. Here's a menu. Help yourself. We don't usually get busy until about seven."

"Thanks." I wound my way around the hostess's lectern and up two steps passing tables whose polyurethane shined so thick I could have put my makeup on in the reflection. I plopped down on a green-leather barstool and began searching through the items on the menu for something light but filling. Within a moment of my closing the menu, the bartender arrived.

He was old enough to be my grandfather. He had a protruding beer belly and a receding gray hairline. He fit the stereotype of the perfect New England curmudgeon except for his thick Irish brogue. "What can I get for you, lassie?"

"I'll have stuffed baked potato skins with sour cream, fried cheese sticks, and a Diet Coke, please."

"That's an awful lot for a little person like you. You might as well add on an ice cream soda to top it off."

My cheeks reddened. I knew I had a penchant for fried food, but since my waistline didn't notice, I never saw any reason to change my dietary habits. "No. The Diet Coke will be just fine, thanks."

The bartender grabbed a tall glass, filled it with ice and soda and set it in front of me with a chuckle. "The skins and cheese sticks will be right up."

To pass the time and resist the urge to eat the entire basket of peanuts sitting in front of me, I opened the pictures on my cell phone to see if I could make sense of something I found in the calendar. The images were small and difficult to read, but I could make out a few handwritten words: staff meeting, Finnigan's, and under another Finnigan's entry was "Captain Omnipotence"—or that's how it looked. I studied those and some other kooky, nonsensical words such as "The Celebrated Learn" and "It a Gang." These phrases appeared more than once, or so I thought, but I couldn't be sure, the images were so small and fuzzy and the words so cryptic. I hoped when I returned home and opened my email, I could work with clearer images and the entries would make more sense. The bartender must have noticed my predicament.

"Whatever you're looking at must be pretty important for you to be squinting your eyes up like that," he said. "All this new fandangled stuff, I don't know what you young people see in it. We got along just fine without it when I was growing up."

"I know what you mean. You don't think you need it until you get it, and then you can't live without it." I paused, noticing him taking an interest in exactly how it worked. "See, it's just a cell phone that takes pictures. Then you can send them to your email address if you want to." Turning the camera around I said, "Watch, I'll take a picture of you." I snapped the shutter and turned the phone to show him.

He shook his head in dismay. "Whatever happened to thirty-five-millimeter film?" he asked. "There was a guy in here the other day with this thing about the size of my hand. I think he was making stock exchanges or something. Me, I just stick with what I know." He tapped the top of the beer taps.

"Oh, they still make film. I think." I smiled, closing the camera and putting the cell phone away. "I should introduce myself." I offered him my hand. "I'm Morgan Langdon."

"I'm Patrick. Patrick Finnigan, owner of this here establishment. Nice to make your acquaintance."

The increased buzzing of conversations and the number of bodies filling up the stools at the bar confirmed that the busy hour was beginning. "Looks like business is picking up. It usually does this time of day," he said.

"You have a nice place. I can see why Emile Voorhees liked to come here." I had no idea if that name would ring a bell, but there was no harm in trying.

"You knew Mr. Voorhees? A nice girl like you?"

Blushing, I explained. "Not personally. He and his wife are members at my yacht club in Harbor View, Rhode Island. I was there the night he died."

"Dead, huh? Think I heard something about that. I'm surprised he wasn't bumped off years ago."

"Technically he wasn't bumped off. He died under suspicious circumstances or so they say."

"Suspicious, huh? It doesn't matter to me how he went, lassie. He was a crook and a philanderer and I don't have any sympathy for those types." Then he muttered what sounded like an Irish curse: *Imeacht gan teacht ort.*

I assumed that was meant for Emile, not for me. "Should I dare ask what that means?" I said.

"I would always curse to him under my breath when he left. It's Irish for 'may you leave without returning'." He wiped his white towel in circular motions up and down the length of the oak bar before returning to me. He leaned across the bar and whispered, "I'm not one for gossip, but that man had a lot of seamy visits with men *and* women. He used to sit right over there." He pointed to a solitary booth built into a corner near the back. "I knew things weren't on the up and up, but he was always polite and paid his bill, so what was I to do? I'm just glad to see him gone."

I raised an eyebrow at Mr. Finnigan.

He squirmed in his brown leather boots. With a polite tone he added, "Not that I meant him any ill will."

"Of course not. Let me ask you, does the name Captain Omnipotence mean anything to you? It seems Mr. Voorhees used to meet someone here with that name on a regular basis. I thought maybe he captained a fishing boat down here."

"Like I said, Voorhees met a lot of people. Enough of this chin-wagging." A bell dinged from the back and Finnigan excused himself. I hoped it was to fetch my fried culinary delights because any minute now my stomach would begin to notify anyone within earshot it was time to eat.

The owner arrived back with my dinner just as a young bartender, probably in his twenties, was coming on duty.

"I'm finished for the day," Finnigan said. "Bones as old as mine can't work as long as they use to, but Shawn, my grandson here, will take good care of you. It was nice meeting you." He slipped off his apron and pushed it under the counter, shoulder-slapped Shawn good-bye and left out the back door.

Ten minutes passed. Shawn was busier than an octopus in a shrimp farm, but eventually he stopped in front of me and asked if I'd like a refill of my Coke.

"Thanks. You're grandfather's a nice guy. How is it to work for him?"

"Okay, I guess. He's a bit too old-school for me, but I suppose that's the way his generation is."

Not wanting to reveal the specific reasons I came, I asked, "An acquaintance of mine, Emile Voorhees, used to frequent your bar with someone called Captain Omnipotence. Do you know who that is?"

Shawn's face sagged. He glanced nervously toward the other bar patrons and then back at me. He knew something, but I could see from his defensive posture he was not about to let any information slip. “Why, who’s asking?”

Pensively I sipped my soda. “Oh, no one. I just remember hearing Mr. Voorhees mention his name and I was curious.”

“Yeah, well, I don’t know any Voorhees so I wouldn’t know any Captain Anybody either. I’ve gotta get back to work. Do you need anything else?”

I shook my head. As he moved down the bar I made the assumption that it was a very windy day when that apple fell from the tree. I took the last gulp of my soda and wondered why the Voorhees name would elicit such a suspicious response. While I pondered the possibilities, I realized the evening was catching up to me and I caught myself yawning into my drink. I didn’t relish the long drive home alone. Shawn laid the bill for twelve ninety-five down in front of me. I left fifteen dollars. It was almost a twenty percent tip, left mostly for Mr. Finnigan’s politeness.

Moving quickly I exited the main door and strode toward my car, which was parked in a section of the lot lit only by a small light protruding from the back brick wall. Even though I was in a metropolitan district there was minimal light pollution, even the stars and moon seemed to be hiding their illumination. With my keys in hand I walked with awareness and authority toward my vehicle. Such a tactic was supposedly a surefire way for a woman alone to stave off a potential mugger. According to defense specialists, I’ve been told, muggers gravitate more toward women who look meek and defenseless. I carried myself with the confidence of a karate expert, but the intruder must have sensed I didn’t know a black-belt chop from a football play as he approached me from the darkness of an alleyway, stopping me in my tracks.

"I heard you were asking about Voorhees and the captain. Why?"

Who was this person who sounded like a thug, the kind that plays the slimy role on a weekly police series? The details of his face were hidden in the shadows, but I could see his complexion was dark as he lit his cigarette. His leather jacket crinkled as he took a long drag, then flicked the ashes in my direction.

I broke into a sweat as I tried not to let my legs give out on me. I wanted to appear in control of the situation, but I felt like a timid bunny being cornered by a raptor. I tried quelling my fear by directing my gaze away from the mysterious figure. "I'm not looking for anyone. I don't even know any captain. I was just curious."

"Curiosity killed the cat."

This wasn't the first time in the past two weeks I had heard that phrase, but it was starting to hold more meaning, as I stood motionless by my car. "What do you want? Isn't it obvious I don't mean any harm? I'm just a pet store owner from Harbor View." I wondered about the type of punishment he would inflict for my assertiveness.

He shifted, looking behind him and throwing his cigarette to the ground. In the faint beam of available light I saw him place a large biker's boot on the cigarette and twist its ashes into the dirt. "If you know what's good for you you'll keep your curiosity to yourself. You don't want to end up like that poor little kitty. You get my drift?" He didn't wait for a response. Clearly he intended to terrorize not torture. He turned, walked down the side of the building through the alleyway and disappeared like a phantom into the darkness.

I fumbled with my keys, only managing to unlock the door by sheer determination. I had never been so scared in my life, but intimidation angered me and only heightened my desire to learn the truth. I was foolhardy and careless to the point of getting hurt, yes. Nick was always telling me so. Maybe this time he was right.

CHAPTER 12

I shivered. My jagged nerves stayed sharp on the drive home. For the second time that evening my heart felt as if it would explode from my chest cavity and drop to the floor. My cocky ambitions had gotten the best of me. This day should have given me much to ponder, but a warm mug of hot chocolate and my snuggly slippers were the only things on my mind. It was after nine when I pulled into my driveway. I felt somewhat renewed by the glow of a small kitchen light I'd had the foresight to turn on before I left.

I was both surprised and relieved that Nick hadn't tried calling me on the cell phone. Maybe he had left a message at home. I hoped so. I needed his calming voice to still my pounding heart.

Cooper pushed his way out the back door for a much-needed potty break while I changed and put water on to boil. At the precise moment I sank down into my favorite rocker piled with cotton pillows, the phone rang.

The caller identification said the call was coming from Nick's cell phone. Relief swelled through me. "Hi, honey. I really miss you. Did you have a good day learning all about dental laser stuff?"

"You miss me, huh? It usually takes you two days before I get any sentimental remark. What have you been up to?"

"Why are you so suspicious? Can't a wife just miss her husband when he's far away?" I knew at some point I would have to give in and tell him the truth, but for now I kept silent. If I told him everything that had happened to me, he would just worry and want to take the next plane home.

"I still say something's up, but thanks for missing me anyway. I miss you too, and, yes, I've come away with a few interesting tidbits of information." He droned on about the positive aspects of laser dentistry and how much the systems cost and which renowned dentists he had met. I always found Nick's take on dental issues interesting. He could make the dullest activities seem fascinating, but tonight was different. My mind was racing and I wanted to be able to share what I found out, but how?

He must have sensed my disinterest and fatigue. "I'll stop boring you to tears, my Irish Eyes. I'll see you tomorrow. Love you, goodnight." He blew a kiss into the phone and I blew one back, hugging the phone before I replaced it in its cradle. I leaned back, closing my eyes while trying to usher in thoughts of his return.

Forty minutes later I awoke with a start. The image of a deranged figure coming toward me holding a blunt instrument in one hand and a calendar in the other was the remnant left from my fitful nap. If dreams are a twisted form of reality, what is this one trying to tell me? Was I getting closer to the truth? Was my dream scene a haunting portent of the future, like the Ghost of Christmas Yet to Come in *A Christmas Carol*? And why hold a calendar? What secret message did it possess?

Then I remembered the photographs I had emailed from my cell phone. I rushed to the computer, hoping the pictures would look crisp and clear. I moved the mouse, typed my password, double-clicked on the attachments icon and then waited with high expectations as my email program downloaded the information. When the photo screen appeared, I leaned back in my chair wide-eyed and clapped my hands in approval.

"Take a look, Cooper. Your master is really a wizard. Here lie before us the daily events of Emile Voorhees, deceased. I wonder what mysteries these pages hold." Copper twisted his head to the side and licked the laptop. I stroked his head in agreement. "Yes, Cooper, it's a good thing."

I spent the next hour reading and rereading the pages, hoping something would jump out at me—a date, a name, a place—but nothing seemed out of the ordinary. There were consistent entries for certain names and days. He had lunch every Wednesday at one o'clock with his partner. He worked out at the gym three times a week at seven thirty in the morning. Then there were the customary doctor and dental visits. Too bad Nick wasn't his dentist; maybe I would know more. I pictured gassing him before his teeth cleaning and whispering questions into his ear.

Some phrases, such as "It a Gang," appeared for a few weeks or months and then disappeared. "Doc" appeared repeatedly in recent weeks. I wasn't certain it was male or female. There was "Her Clean." This could be a cleaning lady, but why hire one for a few months and then let her go? The name "Captain Omnipotence" showed up every few weeks on Monday night until last January when only the letters CPT.O were noted. I assumed this was the same person, just a shortened version of the name.

These code names had to be a diversionary tactic to keep prying eyes from knowing whom Voorhees was seeing and what he was doing. Why else would he have been so evasive? Certainly CPT.O wasn't some fisherman selling him cod from the pier. And "Her Clean" probably wasn't a janitorial service, either. Talking to his wife again could be helpful. Perhaps these names would have meaning to her.

If a stranger read my calendar, would he or she find enigmatic inconsistencies and discrepancies? Would my schedule read like someone who has secrets or someone who is an open book? I slept a fitful sleep.

CHAPTER 13

Monday, October 21

One of the great things about being a member at Harbor View Yacht Club is the menu in the dining room. Monday through Thursday the club serves dinner from five until nine in the evening. Fridays and Saturdays the dining room stays open until eleven, but the club serves only lunch on Sundays. The food always seems free to me because Nick and I never have to spend cash; we just sign a voucher showing how much we ate that evening. Of course the meals are part of our monthly membership fee. Food service is a use-it-or-lose-it deal for members, so we manage to take advantage of the system and eat at the club whenever the mood hits. Monday night has become a ritual for us, in part because I don't like to cook, but also because there is never a wait at the beginning of the week.

As soon as we had settled in for our usual Monday meal, Art peered around the corner from the kitchen. A few solitary men sat at the bar with drinks but so far Nick and I were the only two customers for dinner. The chef pushed open the hinged door and walked over to our table. "How are the two of you this evening?"

"Not bad. I love this new menu you created. There are some great selections, like this one: cod with toasted hazelnut crust and bleu cheese dressing. Yummy."

"Thanks, that is one of my favorites I brought with me from my restaurant."

"Are you playing chef and waiter tonight?" Nick asked, knowing full well the on-duty waiter was gabbing with the members at the bar.

Art turned to see the young man laughing at some nautical joke one of the older members had told a dozen times. "It's so slow on Monday nights. It's a good night to make merry with the wealthy members. I think Chad keeps hoping he'll win one of them over so he can crew on a boat when racing season begins. As for me, I have the stove and grill heated up and ready to go, but until I get a request there's not much I can do. Thanks for saving me from boredom."

"Can you sit for a moment with us, then? No one else is here. We were going to relax and have a glass of wine before we ordered. Would you like anything?"

Art sat but declined the drink. "On duty and all that," he said." You two go ahead though."

Nick left and went to order drinks. There was always a sports event playing on the television above the bar. Tonight was no exception. *Monday Night Football* would undoubtedly hold Nick's attention for a while.

I looked at Art and shook my head. "Nick may be awhile with the wine," I said.

"It's funny. I used to love watching sports when my daughter and wife were alive, but now sports aren't important to me. I suppose I've changed mostly because my daughter Charlene loved sports too, and we watched games together. Now they just make me sad."

"I'm so sorry, Art. I can't imagine what it must be like to lose your wife and daughter. I'm sure it feels like you've lost a part of yourself."

"A part you never really get back, but like they say, time and work do help. Let's talk about something less depressing. What have you and Nick been up to now that the sailing season is coming to a close?"

It never took much convincing for me to talk about Nick and our businesses. Besides, the combination of dentistry and pet stores just naturally elicits smiles for some reason. I hoped discussing happier topics would lighten Art's mood.

I began telling him about my work and Jessica and the latest quirky customer tales at Paws for Love. One of my favorite stories was the one about the customer who was on vacation and popped in for some crickets. I assumed they were for her lizard or pet snake. I was grabbing a container when I noticed the woman's chest moving as if her breast implants were shifting. Not wanting to stare at her bosom, I distracted myself with scooping up a few crickets. Turning with tub in hand I noticed a tiny striped face with two large eyes gazing at me from between the buttons of the customer's Hawaiian print shirt. I recognized the animal immediately as a sugar glider. I explained to Art that a sugar glider is a creature similar to a flying squirrel, but it's a marsupial native to Australia, although most are now shipped from Indonesia. Mealworms and crickets are their favorite foods. I smiled, but kept silent and gave the lady her bag of insects.

Nick often sees humor in his profession too. When removing impressions trays for dentures or crowns, he tells his patients, "Don't worry. We *almost* always get these out." The material he uses exerts quite a bit of suction when he pulls on the tray, and Nick says the look of concern on a patient's face as he rocks the device is priceless.

Art offered a genuine smile in return for my creative storytelling. I was ready to continue with tales from my latest nursing home visit with Cooper when Nick arrived with my Riesling.

Art stood and pushed his chair under the table. "I'll leave you two alone. Thanks for the chat. I never knew how comical the pet store industry and dentistry could be. Do you two know what you would like or should I send chatty Chad over in a few minutes?"

"No, I'm ready. I'll take the cod with that crusty stuff on it and the finger potatoes," I said.

Nick ordered the same.

Art tipped his chef hat. "Two for cod with toasted hazelnut crust. It'll be ready in about fifteen minutes," he said, smiling as he pushed his way back through the doors to the kitchen.

"How comical dentistry can be? What did you tell him?" Nick gave me his serious doctor glower.

"Oh, don't worry, I didn't embarrass you." I took a long sip from my goblet and added, "I should let you know something, though, before it gets too late."

"What did you do now?" Nick asked with a long sigh

"I invited a couple of people to join us for dessert."

"Oh, that's fine, I don't mind." Nick said with obvious relief.

"It's Frank and Carol." I squeezed my eyes closed and pushed out the words like a horse at the starting gate, "Neither knows the other is coming."

"Oh, good grief."

"Now don't go getting your knickers in a twist. It'll be all right. They really like each other. They're just shy." Nick's lack of a rebuttal told me this could be a very quiet evening, at least between the two of us.

Dinner arrived just when Art said it would, steamy and moist. After the first few bites Nick's demeanor lightened and we conversed about everything from insurance to politics to the weather, taking a circuitous route around my uncontrollable need to meddle. We were wiping the last remnants of dinner off our lips when Frank strolled up to our table.

"Hi. Did I arrive at the right time?"

"Perfect, Frank. We just finished our entrée." Rubbing my belly, I said, "Do you mind if we digest before ordering dessert?" I pulled out a chair and patted the seat beside me.

"I've got all night. Mother took the train to New York City to shop with some friends. She won't be back until tomorrow." I couldn't imagine Mrs. Broward having friends, but that didn't matter, Frank's sense of freedom showed on his face and in his speech patterns. I hadn't noticed a single *l* or *r* out of place. He looked like a child let lose on a playground for the first time.

The waiter arrived and took Frank's order of hot tea and milk. My knees bounced under the table. I was eager for Carol to arrive but worried that the couple might not appreciate my Morgan.com Dating Service scam.

Just when I thought my knees would knock the table over, I saw Carol come through the entry and wave. "Hi, everyone," she said, approaching us. "I didn't know you would be here, Frank. It's great to see you." Without any coaxing Carol sat down beside Frank and gave him a shy sweet smile that made him blush. "This was such a nice idea of yours, Morgan," she said.

I shot Nick my I-told-you-so look and proceeded to revel in my romantic intuitiveness.

The evening passed pleasantly as more club members arrived and the dining room began resonating with the din of conversations and clinking glasses—much to the surprise of Chad, the waiter, who was running back and forth to the kitchen. Art and the hostess stepped in to assist with delivering dinners to the waiting patrons. My plan was working like a charm. Carol and Frank chatted with ease as we all enjoyed dessert, coffee, and the recorded background music.

"I'm surprised it's this busy on a Monday evening," Frank said, "Art's probably wishing he had scheduled more waiters. The way things are looking, we may have to pinch hit for him."

"Being a consummate committee member, I wouldn't have a problem with that. Maybe we should call Susan and see if she'd like to come join us?" Carol said, raising her glass in salute and chuckling.

Preparing to toast a perfect evening, my mood changed suddenly from lighthearted to nervous as I spotted the Tagliannos being seated a couple of tables away. The sip of wine I had just taken rolled hard against my tongue and down the wrong pipe, making me cough up half of what I swallowed.

My husband and friends saw the exaggerated cough and turned to glimpse what had caused the upheaval. Carol was oblivious, but Nick and Frank both shot me a look of concern.

"How did your visit go the other day?" Frank asked. Then realizing he might have blundered, he cleared his throat and excused himself to the bar.

I halted him in his tracks. "Sit back down. Listen, you two," I said, addressing Nick and Frank, "here's the thick and thin of it. So what if Mr. T. found out I was at his house and was perturbed about my meddling and felt he had to let me know about it by coming to Paws and threatening me? It's over. Closed book."

Nick's face reddened with frustration until he finally popped like a smashed blood gorged tick. "Have you given one ounce of thought to what you're doing? Have you bothered asking your editor if he's even interested in the Voorhees story? Have you given any consideration to the danger you may be putting yourself in with a murderer on the loose?"

I gestured, patting my hand toward the ground for him to lower his voice. In an audible whisper I said, "Ah hah. You do think he was murdered. Let me tell you something else I found out. Then you'll definitely know I'm onto something." I was about to admit to Nick all I'd done while he was away. The admission at some point in time was inevitable. I couldn't keep anything from him for very long. I hoped that the presence of friends would mitigate any displays of total exasperation.

By now I had the entire table riveted to my words. Carol was wide-eyed. Frank looked pensive. Nick was horrified at the prospects of the undeniable truth finally coming out of his obstinate wife.

I first explained what I knew about the toxicology report. I then described my trip to Boston in vivid detail. I even left in my encounter with the dark figure in the parking lot. I summarized my visits to Barbara Voorhees and Gina Taglianno in a few sentences. I finished with, "I'll talk to my editor this week and if everything pans out, I'll have the story of the decade sitting in my lap."

Nick pushed his chair back. He gripped the table with both hands as he yawed like a sailboat in a stiff wind. "Is there anything else you need to let me know before I kill you myself? I mean, why give someone else the chance?" He exhaled a long breath. "Why do you insist on putting yourself into these dangerous circumstances?"

"Don't over-dramatize, honey," I said. The six eyes staring at me with a determined gaze made me rephrase my response. "What I mean is, there is more to this than meets the eye."

"I've mentioned this before. Maybe you should go to the police with all of this information," Frank said.

"I agree." Carol added.

"I third that and the ayes have it. You're going to your friend on the force this week and let him know what happened if I have to drag you myself." Nick's pigheadedness was clear: go or else.

CHAPTER 14

Tuesday, October 22

Tuesday's workday came and went. I left the shop an hour early to run household errands. There was laundry piled up as high as my head, but no laundry detergent, and half a box of cereal in the cupboard, but no milk. It was a domestic duty nightmare. I left the store in the somewhat capable hands of Jessica who would close for the evening. I kept my fingers crossed she could manage the end-of-day receipts.

It was almost six thirty and I arrived home hauling fourteen bags of provisions to keep us clean, comfortable and content for at least another week. "Hey, Nick, come out to the car and help me with these bags."

Nick was practicing his putting in the family room off the kitchen. His imagination was noisy with cheers from the crowd as he knocked in a birdie for the win at Augusta. He never heard my call for assistance.

"Hey, Nick. That was a great putt, but can you come grab some bags from the car?"

He jumped in surprise and embarrassment. He moved the furniture back in place and stripped himself of his ball cap and golf glove. "Sorry. I didn't hear you. I was practicing."

"I could see that, Nick 'The Shark' Langdon."

His response was a long sneer.

The garage was cold and damp. We decided to maneuver all the bags into four arms and four hands so we didn't have to make another trip. This took about five minutes, a bit of polite cursing and some laughter before we managed to close the trunk and make our way back inside.

Cooper was waiting at the door, pacing back and forth to the kitchen counter, a behavior that usually meant someone had left a message on the answering machine. It made him antsy, I think because he could hear the voice but not see the person attached to it.

I pushed the 'play' button and heard Jessica bantering. "Thought you might want to know I had a problem with the deposit this evening. The total was off a couple of bucks. You might want to check it before you take it to the bank in the morning. Sorry about that. Hope you're having a good evening. See ya."

"I would have if you had gotten the deposit right. Good grief."

"How many times does that make this month?" Nick asked, dropping the bags on the floor in front of the sink.

"More times than I can count. I still can't figure out what's so tough about adding up the cash, checks and charges and comparing the total with the day's end receipt. I'm going to have to go in after dinner and fix it. I don't want to have to deal with it in the morning."

"Do you want me to come with you?"

"How about you and Cooper stay and keep the bed warm until I get back."

"What do you say, Coop?" He rolled Cooper's ears around in his hands. "Can we keep the bed warm?" Cooper raised his paw to shake an agreement. "Positive confirmation has been issued by the dog in charge. Now what's for dinner?"

An hour and a half later the leftover chicken enchiladas had been packed in the refrigerator and the dishes had been washed and put away. Ten minutes later my tires crunched across the gravel parking lot at Paws for Love. My eyes had difficulty adjusting to the dim light when I jumped out into the moonless evening. For some unknown reason the back porch light was off. I wondered if Jessica was having a bad night all around and had turned off the dusk 'til dawn light switch. Maybe I was being too hard on her; perhaps the light sensor was broken. I made a mental note to check it and pick up a new one the next day if necessary.

Taking baby steps I groped my way up the back porch to the door. I had a small light on my key chain. It lit up like a lightning bug as I slid the key into the lock. Once inside I fumbled up and down the wall to my left until I felt the light switches. I flipped them back and forth but nothing happened. Muttering an exasperated sigh, I eased my way across the room to my desk. I laid my purse and keys down and leaned over to pull on the lamp chain, but the outcome was the same. Darkness. "Ah, the charm of old buildings. It's probably the fuse box," I said aloud.

I pushed open the swinging doors leading out into the main store. I stopped a moment, tuned to the total silence. An unknown source of sound evoked a prickle of fear that crept up my back and nestled at the nape of my neck. I tried rubbing it away with the palm of my hand. My friends knew it took a lot to scare me. All through high school and college I was the only girl who kept my eyes open during every horror flick and I never once jumped at the scenes that made all the other girls squeal. Part of my cavalier attitude came from being so pragmatic. When my five friends and I rented *Psycho* for the first time and the shower scene arrived, I felt the need to explain how the director used chocolate for the blood because of its realistic consistency. I should have realized my friends wanted to be frightened; they didn't want a lecture on special effects.

I figured the past couple of weeks were getting to me more than I realized. "Focus, Morgan," I said to myself. The fuse box was on the wall inside the stairwell to the basement. I knew what lay in every nook and cranny of my store so I maneuvered with ease in the blackness, rounding the counter and shelving on my way toward the basement steps. My left hand slid across the countertop until I reached the cash register. As I shifted to my right, I was certain I felt the breath of some warm-blooded creature behind me. Had Jessica forgotten to lock all the cages? I hadn't time to finish that thought before I felt my body being twisted around and pushed to the ground. I landed on my knees, catching myself with my hands on the rough-hewn floor. I let out a yelp as my ankle twisted in an unnatural direction. A dark figure pushed its way past me, leaving a whiff of unfamiliar odor behind. I could hear the intruder tripping over the brochure rack and rolling across the floor toward the front door. There he—or she—fiddled with the deadbolt. The glass door banged open with a shove. I heard footsteps running into the night. I lay on the floor, frightened and shocked.

I lifted myself up and felt twinges of pain in my lower back and ankle. The points of a few splinters protruded from my palms. I limped to the fuse box and flipped each circuit breaker back and forth until I saw the back office lights come on. Then I immediately dialed 9-1-1 and Nick.

"You say you found this note attached to your cash register, correct?" Mark Sherman asked.

"Yes. After I turned on the lights I went to check to see if anything had been stolen, but the only thing I found was this note." I held it up by the corner with a piece of tissue in case there were fingerprints. The note was made with colorful letters cut from magazine articles and pasted on a small sheet of poster board. Its' meaning was clear: LeaVe wELL ENough AloNe or ElsE!

"What do you think this means?" Mark's eyes swung like a pendulum between Nick and me. "Are you on a story for the paper?" Nick looked at me, then at the floor. "Someone say something, please."

"I'm not officially on a story, but I'm sure I will be as soon as I show all the facts to my editor."

I could see that Mark sensed some tension between Nick and me. He asked Nick and another police officer to check again for missing items then took me aside for a private talk. "I've read enough of your stories in the paper and offered you enough police advice to know the types of people you can come into contact with. So what is it this time—more puppy mills, dog fighting…nursing home abuse?" He waited with raised eyebrows for a response.

"No…not exactly"

"Now what the heck is that supposed to mean."

"Well, it could be…like possibly…I mean maybe…it's just I think I might be onto…well…it's Emile's murder."

"That was a definitive answer." Mark's sarcasm cut deep. "What do you mean murder, anyway? Death wasn't by stabbing and I told you what the lab has said. How many times do I have to tell you?"

"I've been doing a little journalistic investigation. I can't prove it, but the break-in and this note say to me I'm making someone uncomfortable." I nodded grimly toward the evidence lying on the counter.

"Yeah, maybe too uncomfortable. Listen, I realize there's someone still out there who tried, if unsuccessfully, to murder Voorhees. That may be the person you're making a bit itchy. You need to tell me everything you know and let the police handle it from here, Morgan."

Although I still believed that Voorhees's death was actually murder, it was clear that Sherman wasn't going to believe me until he had substantial proof, either from the lab or me. "Listen, Mark. I'll tell you everything you want to know, but I'm not making any promises about keeping my nose out of things. Investigation is my job."

"It's my job too and according to you, your editor hasn't given you carte blanche to go chasing some nonexistent story. So until he does, you're leaving this case to me, understood?"

I shuffled my feet and managed a slight nod. I knew the promise would be canceled after I spoke to Bob Horton, my editor.

"Back to the task at hand. Do you have any idea who this might have been? Obviously, it's someone who's perturbed at you. Whom have you been talking to since Voorhees's mur…death?" Mark corrected himself before I had a chance.

Nick approached me from the back and interjected, "There's nothing missing that I can see. It's late, lieutenant. Can we finish this tomorrow morning?"

I yawned in agreement. "If you don't mind my waiting on customers, I'd be glad to bring in coffee and croissants in the morning and we can talk as long as you like."

Mark agreed reluctantly, shaking his head in frustration. He and his partner finished dusting for prints, made some last-minute notes about the break-in and stuffed the menacing message into a large envelope. "See you at eight o'clock sharp," Sherman said. He left tipping his baseball cap in my direction.

I had imagined hunting down the clues, serendipitously finding evidence and proudly presenting my findings to my editor for an excellence in journalism award. Never in all my musings had I imagined I would be standing in my store with a broken lock, a sprained ankle, a threatening letter and an irate husband about to chew me out. None of my other freelance stories had been fraught with so much intrigue and dangerous dalliances, but then as sad and horrific as puppy mills and cruel nursing home attendants can be, they, so far, hadn't made any threats against my health and well being. I dug my heels in, ready for the one-two punch from Nick.

"I don't have patients until nine tomorrow morning, so if you don't mind I think I'll come with you to talk to the lieutenant. Afterward you can call your editor and then the four of us will decide how to proceed. Okay?" He emphasized the words 'the four of us' as he placed his arm around my shoulder and escorted me out the back door, shutting off the lights behind us.

Oh dear. Nick's commanding attitude was not a good sign. It could mean I was looking at an ultimatum; which would leave me with little choice in the matter.

CHAPTER 15

Wednesday, October 23

I tossed and turned all night: one, from hashing over the events of the past few weeks: two, because of my aching ankle from the fall. Wednesday morning came all too soon. The sun was topping the horizon and I knew I was duty-bound to tell Mark everything, but how to present what I knew or suspected was the question. The brilliant fall morning dawned with little jubilance. We drove in separate cars to Paws for Love: Nick so he could leave for work from there, and Cooper and I so we could pick up the croissants at the local bakery. We all arrived at the shop as the church clock chimed eight.

I hurried to put on a pot of coffee. My back office was as comfortable as a home. I had placed in one corner an old overstuffed chair I had confiscated from someone's trash and reupholstered. The small paint-chipped table we used for breaks was also a trash find. In addition the tiny kitchen provided the accoutrements any employee would take over a pay-raise: cream for coffee, sugar and boxes of crackers—everything to make a long workday bearable.

Mark broke the silence once we were all seated at the table, coffee and croissants in hand. "Let's start at the beginning. Perhaps you ought to tell me everything you saw and heard at the yacht club party."

"Here's the long and short of it." I began with the conversations I had overheard at the Fall Fest Ball. I told Sherman about my visits with some of the members and I ended with my trip to Voorhees's Boston store. I explained about photographing the man's calendar and told Sherman about the dark stranger who had confronted me in the parking lot. "His last words to me were something about my catlike curiosity." I eyed Nick. "I suppose mentioning to him that I own a pet store in Harbor View was not the best decision I've ever made."

Mark shook his head in disbelief. "I won't even ask what you were thinking when you let that slip. Do you realize how much trouble you could be in for breaking and entering?"

"I didn't break. I just entered."

"You know what I mean. You took privileged information, which wasn't yours to take. You're going to need to hand the photographs over to me. I won't tell anyone unless I have to. As for the tough guy, he sounds like a possible suspect for the break-in, but there's no way of knowing who he is or what he wanted without going to the Boston police for help. Was there any identifying thing you can remember about him?"

"No, other than he must hang out at Finnigan's and be familiar with Voorhees. Why else would he have been so upset at my mentioning Captain Omnipotence—whoever or whatever that is?" I stopped for a moment recalling the night when my life flashed before my eyes.

"Are you remembering something? Morgan, little things might help us track this guy down." Mark looked me in the eyes and waited for a response.

"It's probably nothing. It's almost silly."

"Let me be the judge of that."

"He wore biker boots. You know, the kind with the big silver buckle on the side, and he wore a leather jacket and had a cigarette dangling from his mouth. He was like some fifties caricature. There can't be many like him floating around."

"That's not much, but it's a start. I'll notify the Boston police and see if your description means anything to them. In the meantime I want copies of those cell phone shots. I'll get back to you and until then, please leave things alone." He scolded me with a look as he placed his pad and pencil in his jacket pocket and left.

"I've got to get to the office," Nick said. We can meet for lunch and you can tell me how the conversation went with Bob 'Your Editor' Horton."

No response was needed. I knew what Nick expected of me. We kissed good-bye and I melted into my comfy chair with a large sigh of relief. I looked at Cooper lying at my feet and stroked his thick dark fur to calm my racing heart. He returned a pensive look with his big brown eyes. I knew if he could speak the words would be: don't procrastinate. Just do it.

"All right, already, stop staring at me that way. I'm going to call him." I ambled into the next room, plopped myself on top of my desk and began to dial. On hold, I wondered if Bob had gone down a few pant sizes since my last story. He was about fifty pounds overweight, but sitting behind a desk all day with donuts at the ready wasn't helping him lose any of it.

"Bob Horton. What can I do you for?"

"Hi Bob, it's Morgan Langdon. How've you been?"

"I was just thinking about you. There's been a rash of break-ins at some of the historic mansions. I'm sure you've read about them. We've been doing a few side stories, but I thought this needed more attention. Looks like this would be right up your alley. What do you say, would you like the assignment?"

For a moment I was speechless. Any other time I would have jumped at the chance to go poke around The Breakers and Marble House mansions. If this had been a few weeks ago I would have been ecstatic, but to my mind murder took precedence and I was sure Big Bob would agree after he heard what I had to say. "Normally I would say yes, but I'm working on something else—Emile Voorhees's death, actually—and I think it could be front-page news."

"We've already printed something. Are you saying the suspicious circumstances are not so murky and innocent anymore?

"I have a healthy skepticism based on some facts."

"You've got five minutes. Convince me."

I rattled off the facts as fast as the roadrunner's beep-beep. I took a breath and finished with, "Last night my store was broken into and I was left a threatening letter. 'Leave well enough alone,' it said. Let me prove murder before the coroner's report is final. I've got this feeling and you have to admit, I'm usually right about these things. So what do you think? Is it a go?"

I could hear the tapping of his pencil against his desk. It was his way of plowing through the minutia to get to the heart of the piece. "Have you been to the police about any of this?"

"It just so happens I was discussing this with Lieutenant Mark Sherman this morning and he thinks I may have a point." I hoped I'd be forgiven this small stretch of the truth. "Of course there's nothing concrete from the autopsy yet, but it's just a matter of time." I really believed my own words would come true.

"It sounds like you might have something, but I need facts. Until then, keep anything you find out to yourself. Call me back when the police are ready to charge someone, and I'll give you the lead story. Nice talking to you." He hung up.

I never enjoyed a lengthy hello or a leisurely good-bye from two-hundred-forty-pound Bob. He appreciated a job well done and gave pats on the back when they were deserved, but he could push you out the door as quickly as he could to get on to the next story. His motto was, "Get the facts, get them down, get them out," and that was how he lived every day. I often wondered about his wife and their personal life. I hoped for her sake that he was less rushed at home than at the office.

"Great. Nice talking to you too, Bob," I said to the dead line. Then with a rise of my eyebrows and a scrunch of my cheeks I said, "Well, Cooper, I'd say that's an affirmative response. It's hard to tell though. Bob can be so obtuse, but as far as Nick and Mark are concerned, I've got the green light to find the truth and catch a killer."

CHAPTER 16

Saturday, October 26

My impatience gathered speed the rest of the workweek. I didn't have a moment to call my own. Jessica was out sick with the flu for two days, a shipment of Christmas items came in weeks earlier than they should have and the plumbing was leaking. Anything that could go wrong did. What's more, Nick had three after-hours emergencies. Since his assistant had gone home for the day, I needed to pitch in. The first came when little Jeremy Junket broke yet another front tooth while playing NASCAR in the kitchen. He was the driver, the throw rug was his car and the kitchen cabinet was the wall he hit face first. Wednesday night was a skateboard incident. Concrete is not a friend to teeth. Friday night rolled around and we received a call from Arabella Stratton. A front tooth had fallen out of her denture and she'd swallowed it along with her dinner of pork chops and scalloped potatoes. Her granddaughter's wedding was the next day. She simply had to have her dentures fixed. The week ended with one saving grace. Jessica's temperature was back to normal and she was able to work Saturday morning. I gave her kudos for that.

With Halloween coming soon, I made sure the store had plenty of candy for the costumed kids. I even made dog treats to hand out. I couldn't cook much, but I could manage pre-made biscuits dipped in carob. Dogs loved them. Today Cooper and I would be costumed too, he as a bee, replete with antennae, and I as a giant flower. I didn't realize how much we had been missed the previous Saturday until we arrived at the nursing home. Patients grabbed at our hands and paws, not wanting us to leave. They kept caressing Cooper repeatedly as if they would never see him again. I felt guilty for the sadness I had caused canceling our usual visit just to take a fact-finding trip to Boston. I hadn't realized that a missed visit would create such a stir. It was nice to know we were making a difference, but I felt the weight of the emotional responsibility. Was I doing too much I wondered, as I pulled into my driveway after the end of my volunteer shift.

Nick opened the back door wearing his favorite Steelers sweatshirt and black sweatpants. "Look at the two of you." He chuckled out loud. "How did your visit go?"

"Good, I guess. Everyone really missed us. I felt so guilty."

"Maybe it's a sign you should be more attentive to volunteering instead of investigating."

"Yes," I said. "And the relevance of that remark would be what?" I stopped, controlling the urge to retaliate.

"That you should stop your so called active homicide investigation."

I bit my tongue. I decided a calm, monotone voice was preferable to screaming. I took a deep breath. "How many times do we have to go over this? I am what I am—not only a store owner but also a part-time reporter. I investigate. Besides, Bob Horton gave me the go-ahead."

The silence that followed contained some unexpressed expletives from Nick.

"Let's just drop it for now," I said. "No one's going to win this discussion, no matter what way you look at it."

"What's to win?" he replied. "I'm just trying to make a point. And your editor is not the be-all-and-end-all."

We left it at that, but a chill hung between us for about fifteen minutes until the phone rang. Nick jumped to respond. He was silent for a moment, showing no signs of emotion or recognition. He laid the receiver down, hesitated for a moment and called to me. “It’s Frank. He wants to tell you something.” Nick handed me the receiver and sat down at the kitchen table, keeping his head and eyes lowered.

Listening to the voice at the other end I felt a growing trepidation. With one hand on the phone and the other on the table, I lowered myself to a chair. “How can this be? Explain to me again what you were told and when this was.”

“I went to the yacht club *wate* this morning, about eleven thirty or so. Carol invited me to lunch with her on her boat. When I arrived I noticed a lot of police and rescue vehicles parked near the back toward the piers. I saw your *powice* friend through the crowd, so I asked him what was *wong* . . . and, well, he told me they had found Susan Fairfield’s body floating near her boat an hour earlier. I feel *tewwible*. I never liked the woman, but I’d never wished her dead.”

“What did they say happened?”

“A*ppawentwy* they think she had a few too many last night, *swipped* and hit her head on the winch and fell off and *dwowned.* What a *tewwible* way to go, but I suppose anyway you die is a *tewwible* way. *Wisten,* I just wanted you to hear it from me. We’ll talk later.” He hung up leaving me dumbfounded.

I looked at Nick. We stood and hugged each other, apologizing for being snippy.

“It’s such a cliché, but life really is fragile,” he said. “We should never take any moment for granted.” We kissed and for a nanosecond Harbor View was a safe and happy place to be.

The evening passed normally enough, except for the undeniable truth. Death had visited my town twice in less than three weeks, and this second death seemed as suspicious to me as the first. Tomorrow I would call Mark Sherman and stop by the yacht club, if only to satisfy my curiosity.

Sunday, October 27

The next day in church, Nick and I said a quiet prayer for Susan, her family and her friends. I wasn't sure who they were or if any actually existed, but the thought was there nonetheless. After church we stopped for fish and chips. Nothing quite quelled depression like thirty grams of fat. I bit deep into mine, savoring every juicy bite.

"Honey, doesn't it seem absurd for someone as smart as Susan to let herself get tipsy…at night…alone…with water all around?" I asked.

"What are you getting at or maybe I shouldn't ask." Nick eyed me gravely.

"I know well enough how you feel about my freelance job and the baggage that goes with it, but you knew when we got married how I felt about righting wrongs, getting at the truth, supplanting the unjust. You know, all that Superman-Dick-Tracy kind of stuff." I paused not knowing myself where I was going. "A murder happened at Harbor View Yacht Club three weeks ago and a part of me thinks the same can be said of what happened to Susan yesterday. And as much as I would like to let go of my hunch and pretend my suspicions are nothing, I can't. Because if I give up, I'll be helping a killer get away with murder and I couldn't live with myself if that happened." I hoped my speech would convince Nick.

"That was quite a speech," he said, leaning back in his chair and crossing his arms across his chest. "I could almost hear the national anthem playing in the background." He took a deep breath. "Okay, okay, I'm sorry. Believe me, I do know who and what I married. It's just that I never imagined I would be having nightmares about my wife's part-time job."

Being open and honest may not always be the best policy. I felt my body—along with my pride—slip farther down into the plastic seat.

"I'm only going to say this once and I hope I never say it again." He shook his head and closed his eyes as I waited, uncertain of his response. "I think you're right. Right, at least, about Emile Voorhees, and if finding his killer will make this world a safer place, and if doing so requires your tenacity and intuition, then I'll support you." Before I had a chance to jump up and kiss him, he added, "But there are going to be a few rules from here on out."

I listened with anxious anticipation as Nick laid out all his 'and-if' scenarios and policies. First, I must inform him and the police every time I uncovered something, no matter how small it seemed. I was never to go back to Tagliannos' house unless a full police force accompanied me. And last, but certainly not least, I could not go investigating alone, ever again! If Mark or Frank couldn't go with me, than Nick would go along himself. That was a promise.

I agreed wholeheartedly. I felt safer knowing Nick was behind me one hundred percent. Now at least I wouldn't have to hide things from him. Maybe his input would help.

"I knew you were still the man I married, brave, strong and, of course, handsome." I squeezed his hand and refrained from issuing an I-knew-you-would-come-around statement.

He blew me a kiss.

"Since you appear to be on my side now, how about we," I placed the word in quotation marks with my fingers, "give Mark a call and go to the yacht club. I would like to see for myself how Susan, allegedly, fell off her boat."

While in the car I phoned Mark on his cell to gather any pertinent information and to ask him if we were allowed to go onto Susan's boat. He agreed, saying he would meet us when he was through dining out with his mother-in-law. Unfortunately for him the meal was a weekly ritual, which he was glad to have an excuse to cut short.

Nick and I arrived a few minutes before Mark. The club was quiet this time of year; there wasn't much activity out on the docks. We paused at the shoreline, taking a solemn moment to reflect. "These past few weeks seem surreal to me," I said. "It's one thing to deal with crime when it happens to a name you can't put a face to, but this is different. We both knew Susan. We may not have liked her much, but she was so young and talented. I wonder when the funeral will be. We should make a point of being there."

"I agree," Nick said. "Let's go take a quick look. Those clouds might let loose some rain any second." Nick held my hand as we walked down the dock. The wind was churning the ocean water enough that the dock rocked like a baby's cradle under our feet.

We grabbed at the stanchion on the stern to hoist ourselves inside the cockpit. I stood in the middle of Susan's boat, turning in all directions, noting anything that seemed out of place. The police must have locked the cabin door when they left the scene on Saturday for the padlock was in place. I wondered how much was moved or disrupted Saturday morning by whomever was on board. The ropes lay askew on the deck and the cockpit table was left in an upright position.

"Hey there, you two." Mark waved and jumped on board. "See anything we might have missed? You have a pretty good eye for these things, Morgan."

"You know me. It's more a feeling than anything concrete."

"Woman's intuition isn't always given the credit it's due. My wife tells me that all the time. I brought the report and some photos just in case you might be interested. We've listed Susan's death as accidental. It appears she was drinking, hit her head on the winch, fell off the boat and drowned." He pulled a copy of the report and a few eight-by-ten glossies from a plastic sleeve. "Check these out and let me know what you think." He handed me the information.

"Do you happen to have the key?" I pointed to the padlock. "I wouldn't mind going below to check things out and warm up a bit." I rubbed my forearms.

"We found the key dangling in the lock and the door wide open, so we locked her up. I've got the key here in my pocket somewhere." Fumbling through his pockets he found it and reached passed my shoulders to open it.

I slipped inside out of the wind. Mark and Nick started a conversation beginning with, "Did you see that play Roethlisberger made the other day?" My mind tuned them out and tuned itself into the pictures, the report and the condition of the cabin. Time of death was somewhere between late Friday evening and early Saturday morning. The photos showed a small amount of wine left in a bottle of chardonnay, along with one glass sitting out near the ship's wheel. I made the assumption that a bottle of wine inside a size-four figure might cause some dizziness. Remnants of blood had been found on the portside winch and on the decking. Nothing appeared stolen or in disarray. The wine glass had a ship's knot etched in the side. I searched through the galley cabinets, looking for the rest of the set. The cabinet to the left of the sink held eleven similar wine glasses each with a separate ship's knot. Perhaps she was alone all evening

I sat down to read the police report as I tried to envision myself in Susan's shoes, living the last moments of her life:

> *I purchased a bottle of dry chardonnay at the club bar when I first arrived. It was late, but I needed to relax. Work had taken its toll on my nerves. There were a few patrons left dining and drinking inside, but no one greeted me as I walked down the dock to my boat. I unlocked her and went below, turning on lights in the main cabin. I opened the bottle and removed a wine glass from the cabinet, returning the corkscrew to its proper niche. I tuned the boat's radio to a jazz station out of Boston, grabbed a flannel blanket from my berth and went up top. It was about ten o'clock as I sat drinking alone. I finished most of the wine before I stood to go below. Something or someone caught my attention. I pulled myself up to the port side, but lost my balance. Slipping I grabbed at the stanchion line as I went down, hitting my head hard on the metal winch below me. My world blackened as I dropped off the side into the cold dark water. I wondered if this was a better place to be.*

I had let my imagination get the best of me. I stood up, the papers falling from my lap, a single tear slipping down my cheek. "I swear, Susan, I'm going to find out what caused this so-called accident, one way or the other."

CHAPTER 17

"Are you all right, honey? You look a little pale. Maybe we should go inside the club house." Nick gave me a pat on the back as I hauled myself up the steps from the galley.

"Sure, that would work," I muttered. Nick and I made our way back up the dock with Mark Sherman following close behind.

We sat at a table by the windows–in part for the view, but also to assess how well one could see Susan's boat from the club.

"Did your men happen to mention if music was playing on her boat when they arrived?" I asked Mark.

"I can double-check the report, but I don't remember seeing any mention of it. Why?" he replied.

"Maybe nothing, but it was one of the first things she always did. Turn on her music. We always knew she was on her boat when we heard the music. Why would last night be any different? She's hooked up to electricity so it's not as if her battery could have died." I paused looking down the dock. "This just doesn't feel right."

We all sat in silence for a moment until I spoke again. "I know it was late, but it was a Friday night. I can't believe no one saw or heard anything. Did your guys speak to everyone here that night?"

"As far as I know they tracked down everyone," Mark said. We used the meal and drink vouchers. It doesn't mean there couldn't have been others here on their boats. My officers spoke to all five employees who were working. They say they didn't notice anything out of the ordinary. The bartender remembers Susan purchasing the wine. He said she seemed a bit on edge, but that wasn't unusual from what I've heard. She could be a cold fish. Those are his words, not mine."

"Did someone check to see if any other people were on their boats? Most people would sit below because of the weather. I can get a list of all the members who have slips near Susan's. Maybe someone saw something that could help."

"That's a good idea. Now you've gotten some of your questions answered, do you feel better about this accident?" Mark's reserved tone was sincere.

I sat back in my chair, placing my cupped hands on the linen tablecloth. I wasn't sure there was much to say if he wanted specifics. What I had was more a call to caution then a call to action. Women's intuition means nothing without the facts to back it up.

Nick waved his hands in front of my face. "Hello, earth to Morgan. Where are you? Art just asked if he could do anything for you."

I looked up and saw the head chef waiting solicitously by my elbow. I hadn't even noticed his arrival at our table.

"Oh, I'm sorry. I was off in never land somewhere. How are you doing?" I asked Art.

"A bit shaken. I'm beginning to feel as if I belong on some late night crime scene show."

"Did you see or notice anything Friday night?" I asked.

"Not a thing," Art replied. "I wish I could be more help, but I was in the back most of the night. The docks were totally dark when I left about midnight. Listen, can I get you three anything to drink or maybe an appetizer?"

We all opted for hot chocolate. Art gave the order to the waiter. A few minutes later the hot, sweet drink appeared before me. I chugged mine and wiped the corner of my mouth with the back of my hand. The sugar and chocolate high gave me the sustenance I needed to thrash through all of my maddening feelings.

"Did you notice the way her lines were laid out? They were the same way in the crime scene photos." I searched Nick and Mark's eyes. "You remember, Nick, how I told you Susan always wound her lines in a perfectly symmetrical circle. But in the photographs both the starboard and the port jib lines are a mess. The report said she worked on Friday, so she couldn't have been out sailing. Even if she had been, I'm sure she would have left her lines in perfect order. Speaking of order, I noticed an upside-down wine glass." I nodded sharply toward Mark to imply a significant clue. Nick and Mark gave me a what-are-you-talking-about look. "I believe someone was on board with her last night, but who is the question. A murderer or a friend?" I tapped my finger on the table while I stared down at the docks.

"I do have to admit it seems a bit odd, this time of year, for her to come down here alone, late at night, to finish off a bottle of wine. Why not just go home after a long day's work or at least drink with friends? Do you think she had a drinking problem? Alcoholics will drink alone." Mark couldn't rule out the obvious.

"She could drink a lot but she held it well," I answered. "Maybe she was depressed and felt responsible for Voorhees's death. Could this have been an I-don't-have-anything-to-live-for drinking binge?" I said the words, but I didn't believe them.

"Anything's possible I suppose, especially if she's the one who rammed the knife into his back. We're going round in circles here. As far as I can tell Susan's death was an unfortunate accident. So, if there's nothing else, I really need to get going. Call me when you get the members' list together. I'll have an officer get on those phone calls, although I really don't think they'll make a difference." Sherman took a last sip of cocoa and left by the back door.

I stood, walked to the window and pressed my face against the glass. Lifting my index finger I began pointing back and forth, moving silent lips in time to the rhythm of my hand.

"What are you doing?" Nick approached.

"I'm counting boats to see where I should start the list. Maybe I could call everyone on docks three and four who hasn't dry-docked their boat yet. That way we'll be sure."

"*You'll* call? No, the lieutenant's people will call and you'll wait for the results."

"Nick, I can't get into any trouble making phone calls from home. Besides, these people may be more likely to talk to me than to a policeman, don't you think?"

"I agree to the latter, not the former."

I squeezed his ruddy cheek between my fingers. "You're so adorable and affable when you want to be. Now, you go watch ESPN while I go back to the office and print off what I need." I kissed him and skipped off across the wide room and down the hall.

I turned on the club secretary's computer and brought up the list of all the members who owned a boat slipped at docks three and four. There were thirty-two in all. I highlighted the names of those whose boats were still in the water. That cut the list to twenty-one. I clicked on the button to make one copy and pushed "print." A dialogue box popped up and informed me the printer was out of paper.

I opened a cabinet I had seen paper in the night of the party, but I found nothing. Good grief, I thought, wouldn't you keep the paper next to the printer or does that make too much sense? I decided to check the other offices. Surely someone would have a few blank sheets of paper lying around. I went out into the hall. An enticing aroma wafted from the kitchen. I decided to make a slight detour. I moved down the hall. The last door on the left opened into the back of the kitchen. Art and the part-time help were scurrying about with late lunch orders. I didn't want to disturb them and I didn't see any delectable food within easy reach. I did notice two doors off the kitchen, one leading to the assistant manager's office the other opening into a windowless storage space. That door was open, and was filled with cases of wine, linens and kitchen paraphernalia. The other door was closed.

I moved across the hall to Art's office, where Emile Voorhees had died. I hadn't been inside since the day after the ball. The crime scene tape had long been removed. The space seemed less menacing now than it had then. For an office, it was a large space. Walnut-stained Bermuda blinds covered two windows. The blinds had been pulled halfway up, allowing a view of the docks and the water in the distance.

Art's desktop was in disorder, with recent issues of *Bon Appetit* and *Gourmet* scattered among piles of ledgers, receipts and order forms. On the far-right corner stood a framed picture of Art with one arm around a woman with generous laugh lines crinkling around her eyes and his other arm around an attractive young woman who was flashing a brilliant smile. A sparkling sterling silver necklace hung around her neck. I could see a family resemblance between the young woman and her parents. This must have been Art's wife and daughter. I hoped the picture brought back happy memories for him, not sad ones.

I began to rummage through his desk and drawers until I found some legal-size paper.

"This'll work," I said out loud then startled myself with a small gasp when I turned to find Art staring at me from the open doorway.

"Is there something I can help you with, Morgan?" His glare made me uncomfortable.

"I'm sorry. I suppose I should have asked for permission. I was searching for some paper. Can you believe the secretary doesn't have any in her office? I thought maybe you would. Have some paper, that is." I felt like a kid caught shoplifting a candy bar.

Art relaxed his stiffened shoulders. "No problem. I can see you found some. Is that all you need?"

"Yes. I'll be getting out of your hair now. Thanks."

He turned, giving me enough space to squeeze by before reaching out and placing a hand on my shoulder. "Why are you in urgent need of paper on a Sunday?"

"The lieutenant and I thought it might be beneficial to call the members who moor their boats near Susan's…in case someone may have been on board Friday night and seen something that could answer some questions."

"Questions about what? I thought Susan's death was an accident."

"You know how the police and the newspapers are: they want all the facts. I'll let you get back to work." I turned, forcing him to release his hold.

Within an hour I had printed the list, called Mark, ordered pizza and stationed myself at my home phone, licking cheese from my fingers between calls.

"Hello, Mrs. Deibler, this is Morgan Langdon. I'm a member of Harbor View Yacht Club. You may not have heard yet but Susan Fairfield, who owned *Resuscitate*, drowned after falling from her boat Friday night and I'm doing a follow-up piece on her death for the *Newport Journal.* I was wondering if you could answer a few questions for me." I repeated this same spiel nine times without hitting pay dirt. Then I reached Mr. Francis Cupnik.

"Drowned, you say? I think my wife read about that in the paper. That's terrible, but how can I help?"

"I was wondering if you were on board your boat last Friday night."

"Let me think." He paused. "Yes, I was, but I'm not sure how I can help you."

"Did you see or hear anything out of the ordinary? A stranger, a nonmember lurking about?" I wasn't sure myself what would be significant information, but I hoped when I heard something important, I would know.

"I can tell you why I was down there so late. My wife left a jacket there middle of last week. It's one of her favorites, some kind of mohair something or other with fringe on it. You know how women can be. My wife always says every thing's an accessory, even her coat. So, when she was picking out an outfit for a party we were going to on Saturday afternoon, she just had to have that jacket."

This was more information than I needed and it wasn't helping me get closer to the truth, but I held on resolutely as Cupnik continued. "'Sweetums,' she said, at ten o'clock Friday night, 'can you go fetch my jacket off the boat?' My first thought was absolutely not, but knowing my wife she'd have me trying on outfit after outfit until she decided I would look acceptable for this silly party. So I decided going to the boat was a better alternative."

Trying to sidestep any more specifics on the couple's personal issues, I said, "What time did you go on board?"

"Oh, I'd say about ten thirty. I went down under, closed her up and started tinkering on my hand-held marine radio. It's a VHF 725 Garmin and it's waterproof. This things got ten weather channels and an automatic weather alert that will interrupt a transmission during normal operation if need be. What I really love is the knob-less design that…"

He droned on until my normal patience level was worn down to the size of a gnat. If this was all he could offer and I still had eleven more phone calls to make, I'd be there until the fourth of never. "Mr. Cupnik, I can appreciate the performance of a good hand-held radio as well as the next person, but what I really need is information leading to…" I caught myself before I revealed too much and rephrased, "…helping me write a better story for the paper. Can you please tell me, did you see or hear anything out of the ordinary?"

"No need to get huffy. Let me see." He took a long breath and hummed as he exhaled. "Now that you mention it, when I was standing below I did notice someone walking down toward her boat. I think it was a woman. I'm only saying that because most men don't wear long capes with hoods. Besides there was a kind of wiggle in the walk if you know what I mean."

"I know what you mean. Is there anything else? Did you hear any arguing or loud voices?"

"Can't say I did. Not even sure if the person actually went the whole way down to the doctor's boat. If my wife had been on board you'd know a lot more. She likes keeping up with things. I do know this person left at about eleven, though, because my wife called me on my cell phone wondering what was taking so long. I can't even get thirty minutes to myself without her nagging. I was locking up when I turned and saw the visitor near the end of the pier. That's about it."

"Thanks. That was very helpful, Mr. Cupnik. Enjoy your new radio." I was thankful to hang up. My receiver hand was beginning to tingle. His digressions were worth the outcome, however. I knew that someone else had been on the dock. If the visitor wasn't a suspect, at least he or she might know something.

I finished my list without any new results. No one else had been on a boat near Susan's on Friday night. Now I was left with a dark nameless figure to pursue and no real leads to follow. Perhaps another visit to the recent widow would be in order. I didn't have anything to lose. The worst I could expect was a cold shoulder.

I made a mental note to check with Mark to see if his people had come up with anything on the leather-coated man who had accosted me in the parking lot of Finnigan's. I wondered if somehow all these incidents weren't joined by one common thread from the past few weeks, Emile Voorhees being the thread. And if six degrees of separation means anything, then the dark figure on the dock last Friday night must somehow be connected to it all.

CHAPTER 18

Tuesday, October 29

On occasion the first day of my workweek is good, sometimes not so good. This Tuesday I slammed my toothbrush into its holder. I was in no mood to deal with customers and ledgers today. I took four steps into the bedroom and threw my bathrobe onto the bed. Nick was hurrying about trying to shove his feet into his size-eleven loafers while towel drying his hair at the same time.

I shook my head and sat down. "I'm not going to work today and that's that. I've got to spend some time going over these clues. There is something significant I'm missing, and if I don't come up with some answers, who will?"

Nick sat down beside me. "Stop putting so much pressure on yourself. Mark's got people on this. You're not a police detective, you know."

I stared at Nick in consternation and neither of us knew what to say to the other. I could tell he felt for me and wished he could do more, but his schedule of patients didn't allow him much extra time to spend playing my sleuthing sidekick. "Maybe you should stay home. Can Jessica work for you today?"

"Not the morning hours. I'll have to go in at least until noon, but she could possibly come in at lunch. I think I'll call her."

Twenty minutes later Cooper, Nick and I were all headed out the back door to our designated places of work. "Jessica's coming in at twelve thirty and staying for the rest of the day, thank goodness. I'm not sure what I'm going to do for lunch. I'll call you. Love you." We both waved good-bye through the windshields of our cars, me going one direction, he in the other.

My Volvo squealed into the Paws for Love driveway. I jolted to a stop, just missing the railroad tie that separated the gravel parking lot from the grass. I was ten minutes late for work, but I couldn't imagine anyone would be banging the door down for cat litter or dog biscuits at this time of the morning. Cooper and I ran up the creaking stairs. He sat down to the right of the door and waited to be let in. I turned the key and we both hustled inside. The office was silent and cold, but I knew the chill I felt came from more than the number on the thermostat. I turned the dial to a comfortable seventy-two degrees and took an hour to feed, clean and play with my live inventory.

My mind focused on faces and conversations, not organization and paperwork. After the mandatory labor was done, Cooper and I plopped ourselves down in the back room where I made my customary cup of hot tea and Cooper chewed on a raw hide. I held one of my favorite bone china teacups Nick and I had found on one of our drives through the Connecticut countryside. As we often did, we had come across an antique store we couldn't resist. I was always compelled by a small inner voice telling me a great treasure lay within. On this particular trip I found a Royal Dalton teacup in a rose chintz print pattern. I had no idea what the cup was worth, but I fell in love with it nonetheless. It now held an esteemed position in an antique yellow-painted cupboard I kept in the shop.

I thought perhaps tea in a proper English cup along with a few chapters of Miss Marple in *A Pocket Full of Rye* might give me some inspiration. I leafed through the pages trying to find where I had left off. Frustrated I laid the book down. I felt as if I were living one of Agatha Christie's stories where misdirection plays a role in the confusion to find a killer. Perhaps I was looking at things upside down or inside out. I needed to eliminate some possibilities and Susan was the first to be taken off the list. I spoke to the only creature willing to give me his undivided attention, Cooper.

"If Susan *was* murdered, and I know that's only conjecture at this point, who would have wanted her dead? I can think of only two suspects." Cooper twisted his head as if waiting for an epiphany. "Voorhees's murderer, because Susan somehow knew too much; or Barbara Voorhees because she found out her husband was having an affair with Susan or some other woman. Of course Barbara Voorhees could be Emile's murderer herself, in which case both murderers are one in the same." I stopped, looking down at Cooper. He had cocked his head and was pawing at my shin. "You think Barbara Voorhees too, don't you, Coop? Perhaps this afternoon would be a good time for a social call. What do you think?" A loud bark was his affirmative response.

Keeping to my promise I called Nick and talked with his receptionist, Laverne. She said he wasn't going to make our usual Tuesday lunch because he was running behind schedule. That was okay, I told her, because I had other plans. I left a message about where I was off to. I told Laverne that Nick was welcome to join me should he get an unexpected cancellation. Fat chance of that!

Mark's cell phone answered with its usual message. "It's not convenient for me to talk right now. Leave a message. I'll get back to you." He was abrupt, but to the point in a polite way.

I left a similar message. "I'm on my way to visit Barbara Voorhees. Call me if you have a problem with that. Bye." Now at least I had done my duty by informing everyone as to my whereabouts.

I turned the shop over to Jessica, grabbed a burger and retraced my route to the Voorheeses' home. I pulled into Barbara's driveway at half past two. Dropping in without calling might be a faux pas, but I wanted to catch her off guard. I was hoping she would be home and I was counting on her magnanimity. If she greeted me with any warmth at all, I planned to show her the list of words from Emile's calendar. If she could shed some light on any of the weird lettering, even if it were only a matchstick's worth, I'd know more than I knew now.

I walked up the steps as before, timid but resolute. I turned the door chime. While I waited for an answer, I pulled my cell phone from my purse and turned the ringer off and the vibrate mode on. I didn't want to be interrupted while in a serious conversation.

I heard Cocoa yip three times before the door swung open. Barbara Voorhees greeted me with a half-hearted hello and a downfallen expression.

"Hi. I was doing some shopping in Newport and thinking about you and I wanted to see how you were doing." That wasn't totally false because I was indeed thinking about her.

With little sincerity Barbara Voorhees replied, "How nice of you. I don't have much time to visit. I was on my way out to run a few errands." We stared, each waiting for the other to back down. I stood my ground, determined.

Perhaps seeing the futility of the situation, Barbara said, "Oh, I suppose I have a few minutes. Would you like a cup of tea?" Waving her arm she escorted me back toward the kitchen. A pad and pen lay on the round wooden kitchen table along with a pile of coupons. She brushed them aside, offering me a chair. "Tea or would you prefer something else?"

"Just a glass of water would be great." I knew I needed something to alleviate the dryness and tightness in my throat. I petted Cocoa, who had proffered a paw as she sat at the foot of my chair. Was it possible a true dog lover could be a killer? Feasible, I supposed, but unimaginable to me. I thanked her for the ice-cold water she served me in a cut-crystal goblet.

"Should I assume you heard about Susan Fairfield?" I asked. "I was so shocked." I put on a look of innocence and turned the glass between my hands, making small water circles on the tabletop.

"I didn't know until I saw a small article in the paper. She was so young," Barbara replied. She picked up the coupons from the table and tucked them into her beige Fendi handbag. "There's been so much sadness in the past few weeks, I was thinking Cocoa and I might take a vacation to get away from it all. My parents own a home in the Florida Keys. I think palm trees and ocean breezes are just the ticket to wash away this depression."

Nervously I yammered, "Oh. Good one. Ocean. Wash away. Sort of a double entendre." I said defining each syllable, "I get it. Yes. Absolutely."

A derisive glance from Barbara revealed that no pun was intended. The woman was merely telling the truth. I hoped my flippancy wouldn't stop her from answering a few more questions. Ask anything. Say something. If she goes to Florida I may lose the one person who can help solve these crimes, and I may lose the murderer herself. But who's to stop her? There's no proof of any crime.

Barbara strode across the slate floor to the coat rack in the corner. She wrestled with a few overcoats, moving them from one peg to the next until she came to a long black-hooded wool cape. Flinging the garment around her shoulders, she turned to me. "You'll have to excuse me, but I really must be going. I have a long list of errands to run before the stores close."

For a moment I saw everything in slow motion. The image of the woman Mr. Cupnik described and Barbara's hooded cape being pulled from its hook fused into one vision. My mouth opened and a small gasp escaped.

Barbara jumped. "Did you see a mouse?"

I coughed, clearing my throat. "No. I just swallowed wrong." I tapped the top of my glass. "Since you're in a hurry let me get to the point. I do have an ulterior motive for stopping by."

She cast me another quick unflinching look.

"I'm doing a short article for the paper about Susan and I want to get some facts straight."

"I'm not sure how I can help you. I really didn't know her all that well."

This was no time for tact; now was the time to be forthright and unswerving. Clichés popped into my head in quick succession. Make a beeline for the truth. Be point-blank with your questions. Hit her head-on. I gulped the last ounce of water left in my glass. "I spoke to everyone who was at the yacht club the night of Susan's death and one witness will testify that he saw a woman in a long black hooded cape walking toward Susan's boat Friday night. A coat very similar to the one you're wearing."

Time stood still. The large hand on the clock hanging above the six-burner stove clicked loudly, while it's small brass pendulum swung back and forth. *Tick tock.* I felt like a character in some hideous Edgar Allen Poe tale. Barbara laid her coat across the chair. *Tick tock.* She walked to the counter where a butcher knife lay cradled in a wooden block. *Tick tock.* She stretched her hand toward the block while staring unfaltering in my direction. *Tick tock.*

Then, as dramatically as the moment had arrived, it ended. Barbara Voorhees reached for the stainless steel teakettle that rested on the back burner. "Are you sure I can't make you a cup of tea? I'll be making some for myself. This could be a long conversation."

I closed my eyes, relaxed into my chair and nodded. What was I thinking that she would have stabbed me in her own kitchen? I decided I needed a trip to the Keys far more than she did.

Barbara prepared tea for us both, then settled into the chair across from me. Her gaze was level, her tone solemn. "They say forgiveness is good for the soul. I decided to see if that is true. I went to confront Susan Friday night about her affair with my husband."

"How did you know she would be on her boat?"

"I had called her earlier at the hospital and asked to meet with her. She suggested her boat because she had chores she needed to do down there. It didn't matter to me where we met, so I agreed. I went there a bit before eleven."

"Did you happen to have a glass of wine with her?"

"Absolutely not. This was no social occasion. I just wanted to vent my feelings and leave." She paused a moment, holding the china cup in two hands. She looked deep into its contents as if searching for an answer. "You know, I love English Breakfast Tea, but Emile preferred coffee. In his office at the Boston store, he had a coffee maker with all the bells and whistles so he could make his own whenever he wanted. He hated drinking from the break-room coffee pot." She paused again in reflection. "You know, I do remember seeing a bottle of wine on the upper deck of Susan's boat."

I hesitated, almost blurting out an admission that I had seen the coffee pot firsthand, but I caught myself and redirected my words. "You do realize your meeting with Susan makes you look very guilty."

"Guilty of what? They say her death was an accident." She dropped her cup into its saucer with a clink.

"The police may be convinced, but I'm not. Maybe your anger from one too many affairs got the best of you." I hoped this wasn't true, both for Barbara's sake and my own.

"That's absurd. I went down to the end of the pier. I never climbed on board. She came up from below, turning off the loud music. I told her I knew about her affair with my husband, but I forgave her because better than anyone, I understood how persuasive Emile could be. He made you feel you were the only woman alive, special, beautiful and unique. It all felt true until he got bored with you. Then Susan said she was sorry and that was it. It felt as if she were dismissing me, as if she wanted or needed me to go, so I did."

"How could you dismiss an affair so easily? Weren't you angry? I know I would have been."

"Susan wasn't the only affair he had over the years. I didn't know every name or face, but there were signs. I was always angry at first, but you need to understand I knew whom I had married. I thought I was lucky getting someone as charismatic and handsome as Emile. But as the years passed I realized I didn't want to be treated like some Bruno Magli shoe he could wear whenever he wanted to show off, then throw to the back of the closet when he was done with it. About a month before Emile's death, I filed for divorce."

"Emile's death must have come as a great relief to you then. Now you won't have to go through the what-belongs-to-whom battle." I hoped I would be forgiven for my brusqueness. I had no time for courtesy. At this point I didn't care if I was tilting at windmills because all I wanted was my story on the front page and a killer behind bars.

"That isn't a problem. We had a prenuptial agreement. He couldn't touch my assets and all I could get out of his business was the fifty-two percent I own in shares. That was the amount in down payment I gave him to start Beauty by Design. He's the one who would have lost. He couldn't touch my inheritance after we were divorced. I wasn't going to fight him over my business shares. I just wanted out."

"How convenient. But Emile seems like the type who would have pushed the boundaries. You mean to tell me he went along with this without an argument? Losing millions might be something to dispute."

"He never had a chance to contest the settlement. He died before the paperwork ever reached his desk." She had stopped making eye contact with me, choosing to look down at the churning whirlpool of milk she had just created in her tea.

I wondered if there was anything left to say. It would be easy to find out if and when she had filed, and if she had, what would be the point of killing him or Susan? It seemed a tidy package. Watching Barbara caressing Cocoa, looking very much the part of a grieving yet resolute widow, I had to believe she was innocent.

"Can you explain one more thing to me?" I hesitated, not knowing how to reveal I had seen her husband's calendar. I chose to skirt the issue. "I had a chance to see your husband's business calendar while doing research for a story. It contained some unusual names, phrases that didn't make any sense." I reached into my pocket and pulled out the list I had made from my cell phone pictures and passed it across the table to Barbara.

She raised it close to her face, her eyes moving across each line. "I'm sorry. Most of this, except for 'Doc,' doesn't mean anything to me."

"You know who that person is?" My heart skipped a beat.

"It was Susan Fairfield."

There went another suspect down the drain. Even if Susan Fairfield were Emile's murderer, she had paid her dues in full by dying.

Seeing my disappointment Barbara added, "I do know Emile was fond of eluding people by using his own codes. He didn't like anyone prying into his private or business life, for obvious reasons." Barbara averted my pitying look. "For instance, 'Ta! Sex Due' is for when the quarterly taxes are due. That's not too difficult to figure out. I think he used that code because he was having an affair with his five-foot-eight redheaded accountant. These other words," she pointed to the paper, "could be something like that, but please don't put that in your story. This is all difficult enough as it is." She handed the list back and pushed her chair away from the table. "I really must be going now if there's nothing else you need."

"Yes, of course. You've been very helpful and I promise to be discreet. I'm sorry about the hardnosed questions. It's the investigative journalist in me. I'll let you run your errands."

Barbara nodded and walked me to the door. "I'm glad you came over. It was good for me to get all this business off my chest. Good luck with your story," she said.

I jumped in the Volvo, wondering whom I would pursue next. Secret codes weren't my strong suit. Were they anyone's except Sherlock Holmes? Too bad I hadn't read more of his stuff. I pulled my cell phone from my purse and turned the ringer back on. The screen was blinking notifying me I had a message. Before I had a chance to check it, the phone rang. Another call came in. It was Nick.

"Hey. I just got the phone message from Laverne. It's been a hectic afternoon. Mark called me and told me he tried to get through to you but couldn't reach you. He left a message, too. He wanted me to try first before he went looking for you. You are fine, aren't you?"

"Yes, I'm fine and I'm pretty certain Barbara is innocent of any crime."

"Thank goodness. I don't want to know what you would have done if she hadn't been."

"Thanks for worrying, honey. And since I don't want you to worry about me for a second time in one day, how about we make an appointment together to visit Richard Taylor and see how the business is running without Emile committing larceny?"

Nick had to know I would go without him, promise or no promise. "How do you feel about fast-food bean burritos and tacos for dinner?" he asked.

CHAPTER 19

Hot sauce rolled down the palm of my hand as I bit into my taco. Cooper lay on the backseat of the car waiting for a handout. Nick had opted for a chicken wrap so he could maneuver bites into his mouth with one hand while driving with the other.

"I still don't understand why you couldn't do this over the phone and does this Richard Taylor know why we're coming tonight after business hours?"

"Body language is all I'm saying and yes and no to the second question." I received a shame-on-you look from Nick. I countered it with, "I told him who I was and that I was doing an article on Emile Voorhees for the paper, which isn't altogether a lie. Just be thankful Taylor's meeting us at his Brockton store and not in Boston. The traffic there is hideous."

"If that's supposed to make me feel better about all of this, it doesn't. Besides, I'm not clear on what you think you're going to get out of him. He wasn't at the club the night Voorhees died. Also what motive would he have to kill Susan, if she was killed and that's still a big if."

"I can't answer the Susan question yet, but the former I can answer in one word: poison."

"You've got to be kidding. Did the coroner's report come back or are you just speculating?"

I thought hard, knowing the tox report saw something irregular. "Poison is the only thing that's makes sense. We know Voorhees didn't die from being bludgeoned or shot or suffocated. What else is there?"

"As it stands, heart attack or some health ailment. If the lab doesn't come up with enough evidence, what you believe isn't going to matter. The toxicology report could still come back and confirm a heart attack. Then how will you twist the facts into another theory?"

"I'm not twisting. I'm surmising." I thought better of my verbs and tried again. "No, it's more than that. It's deductive reasoning. If so many questions do not have obvious or even feasible answers, then that is where the truth must lie."

Nick mimicked fingering a turned-up moustache. "Whatever you say, Hercule. Now hand me my other chicken wrap, please."

The hour's drive flew by as we exchanged speculations on the innocence or guilt of Emile Voorhees's partner. On the one hand Taylor could have slipped Emile a permanent Mickey before the end of the workday. If he had, he had a perfect alibi. He was nowhere near Art's office when Voorhees died and he could not have put the knife in the man's back. On the other hand why resort to murder? Why not hire an investigator, get the facts and take the cheating partner to court? If Emile were defrauding the company, he would have been ousted. A suit might have cost Taylor his savings, but it was safer than risking a murder conviction. But, as Nick pointed out, murderers rarely think about the consequences. No great insight developed before we arrived at Beauty by Design.

"I think you'd better wait for me in the car," I said. I knew Nick would never buy that approach, but I tried anyway.

"Oh, right. Leave you alone with a possible murderer. I don't think so."

"Do you really believe he would kill me knowing you're waiting in the parking lot? And look." I pointed to the store window where we could see an employee with receipts and paperwork laid out on the counter. "There are other people still working."

"The more the merrier. I'm coming in. End of discussion."

We assured Cooper we wouldn't be long. We knocked on the front door to catch the attention of the well-dressed employee. He must have been expecting us because he unlocked the door without hesitation.

"Mr. And Mrs. Langdon, hello. Mr. Taylor is expecting you. He's in his office." He pointed to the back of the store where a door stood open.

I turned to the employee and asked, "Would you mind if my husband stayed out here and looked at your beautiful jewelry? Christmas *is* right around the corner." With a wink and a smile I left Nick fuming, thanked the sale clerk and slipped through the door into the back hall.

I knocked twice at an office door with Richard Taylor's name on it. Getting no response, I opened the door and saw Richard Taylor seated in a swivel chair facing his computer, his back turned to the door.

"Hello, Mr. Taylor. I'm Morgan Langdon with the *Newport Journal.*" He turned and stood up. He appeared congenial in an open-necked oxford shirt and an argyle sweater. He reached out his hand and grasped mine in a welcoming gesture.

"Hello. Come on in and have a seat." He pointed to a dark-brown leather couch. Above it hung pictures of what I guessed to be some of the first advertising campaigns Beauty by Design had ever run. I vaguely recalled a few of them, especially the black-and-white photo depicting a seasoned cosmopolitan couple. They were walking away from the camera. From the gentleman's left hand, which was slipped around the lady's waist, dangled a heart-shaped diamond necklace. The caption read, "Surprise her with something from the heart." Any man who believed chivalry and romance didn't exist anymore could have his mind changed in a nanosecond by one of those billboards. I wondered whether the creativity of Emile's designs or the skill of the advertising agency had made this store profitable.

My wandering mind returned to the here and now when Taylor spoke. "I think it's good that Emile's being recognized for his vision and business savvy. I'll be glad to help with your story in any way I can. Where would you like to start?"

I asked the usual and expected questions, beginning with how the two of them met, what drew them into partnership and how would Beauty by Design go on without its award-winning designer? I received the expected polite responses.

"We met in college." Then correcting his statement he said, "He went to Rhode Island School of Design and I went to Brown for a business degree. We met at a local hangout. He was an outgoing, take-chances kind of guy and I was his practical geek friend. He got the girls and I got to go along for the ride. It wasn't a bad set-up actually. The friendship developed into a business relationship a few years after we graduated. And here's the result." He pointed to the posters hanging above the couch.

"Yes, I see. What will happen now that he's gone? I've heard new designers have already been hired."

"I'm sure that's no surprise to anyone. I am only the money guy; I make sure the funds flow in the right direction. As we go forward with the business, we'll keep the standard of excellence Emile set forth, but every designer places his or her own signature on every piece. Things will be different, but we'll still have a distinctive look that sets us apart from other jewelry stores."

As had happened to me with Barbara, my patience began wearing thin. I wanted to blurt out that I heard him call Emile a smarmy liar, but thought better of it. I didn't want to reveal that I had been hiding under Emile's desk. "It's unusual to see partners whose relationship is so copasetic. I've interviewed others for this article and I got the impression things weren't always smooth sailing for the two of you. How was it working day in and day out with a partner who had such a large ego?"

Taylor shifted in his seat. His body language said he had a story to tell. "His ego was the reason for our partnership. He was talented and handsome and married to one of the wealthiest woman in the area. It was his ego that created all of this."

He could have run for political office, but everyone has a breaking point, and I was about to find his. "I have to tell you I've spoken to some of your employees and they have quite a different take on your relationship, so maybe you would like to set the record straight. Rumors have it Emile had some pretty bad habits like women and drugs and because of that he needed extra cash. Cash he didn't have, until he started exchanging real diamonds for fakes. With him gone, the company, more specifically you, will be better off it seems to me."

Richard Taylor's face turned crimson and his eyes bulged. "What is this, an inquisition? I agreed to an interview not a tabloid lashing." He stood and crossed the room with a deliberate stride, stopping only to open the door. "This interview is over," he said.

"Mr. Taylor, forgive me for my bluntness, but I'm only repeating what I have been told, true or not. If I've heard these rumors then others will too. Don't you want to set the record straight?"

"There's nothing to set straight. Emile wasn't perfect. He had problems, yes, but nothing we couldn't handle. And if you're insinuating I may have had something to do with his death, think again. His share of the company went to his wife and I'm left without a preeminent designer. I was better off with him alive, vices or not. Now if you don't mind, I'd like you to leave."

The air was thick with half-truths and diversionary tactics. "I'm sorry. I just want to get the facts straight for everyone concerned."

"Are you sure about that? It seems to me all you're looking for is sensationalism so you can sell more papers. I'll be sure to cancel my subscription. Now if you'll excuse me."

Nick was pacing the floor in front of the bracelet cabinet when I emerged from the back hall. "I heard raised voices. What were you doing, interviewing or interrogating?"

"The *interview* is over. Come on, Cooper's probably wondering what happened to us." I pulled on Nick's sleeve and rushed him out the front door.

We hunched our shoulders against the cold evening wind. It was spiraling around the parking lot, smacking us hard enough to make us catch our breath as we reached for the door handles.

The drive home was quiet except for a few heavy sighs and one or two groans. After thirty minutes Nick broke the silence. "What's up in that pretty little brain of yours?" he asked. "Maybe if you would explain to me what went on back there I could help you?"

I kept staring through the windshield and offered no reply.

"Hey, talk to me, will you? Do you think he did it or not?"

I wiggled in my seat and turned to face him. "I really don't know. He was Mr. Congeniality at first. Then when I started questioning him about Emile's after-hours interests he got all bent out of shape. If he's got nothing to hide why wouldn't he want to set the record straight?"

"Did you ever think that if Voorhees were snatching real diamonds and replacing them with fakes, Taylor wouldn't want the world to know?" Nick's lips were set in a tight line.

"I suppose, but if he didn't know . . . if Emile *were* going behind his back . . . it's not his fault, is it?" I believe people, in general, are good and decent. I always want to give everyone a fair shake, but I have to concede that many are not so open-minded. The sad truth is that most people would probably assume that Taylor was in cahoots with Voorhees.

"I suppose not," Nick said. "What are we going to do now?"

I left the question unanswered. We drove the last mile home with rain spitting and dancing off the macadam lit by our headlights.

There were three messages on the answering machine when we arrived home: one from my parents inviting us to dinner over the weekend; a second from a patient who thought it was acceptable to call the doctor's home number to tell him she had to cancel her appointment on Wednesday; and a third from Mark Sherman. He hadn't wanted to leave a long message or bother me on my cell, so he simply asked me to call him as soon as I got in.

"Hi, what's up? I just got your message," I said, when I got Sherman on the line. I could almost feel the blood pumping hard through my heart muscle. I didn't want to hear about another death, but I was hoping for some information confirming some of my suspicions.

"I thought you might want to know I talked to the Boston police department. They couldn't be certain, but from your description of your night stalker and the location where you were approached, they think the man is probably a cocaine dealer. He tends to sell to wealthier clients out of upscale restaurants. He's been charged a few times, but nothing seems to stick."

"So, are you thinking what I'm thinking, that Emile was purchasing from him?" I already knew the answer. The rumors had to be true. He was doing drugs and maybe he hadn't paid his debt. Maybe the dealer had decided to exact payment, the permanent kind.

"It would appear so. I don't know why else that man would have confronted you about Voorhees. You must have a guardian angel watching over you. He and his people, so it seems, have been responsible for a few Hoffa-like disappearances. Now do you understand why you shouldn't be investigating on your own?"

"I promise to never go looking for drug cartel people again," I said sarcastically.

"All right, Miss Smarty-pants. You're just sore because you know I'm right. Now tell me, have you found out anything else I should know about?"

I explained my visit with Richard Taylor and that I uncovered nothing in my interview. I said good-bye to Mark each of us resolving not to give up and promising to keep the other informed no matter what.

The wind howled, Cooper yawned and I sat slouched onto a kitchen chair and stared at the refrigerator. "Is it possible mental energy can burn calories because I'm hungry?"

"Still? Two tacos weren't enough?" Nick replied. He was getting a drink of water at the sink.

"That was three hours ago."

"How about a frozen pizza?"

Thirty minutes later I looked up from my plate where I was licking up the last bits of cheese. "Honey?" I batted my eyes.

"Y-e-s." He drew out the word as if it had three syllables. His eyes narrowed, his lips tightened and his shoulders squared. His posture said it all: Out of the question. Nothing doing. Don't even ask me.

I asked anyway. "You know there is someone else we need to speak to, whether you like it or not. We don't have a choice. They could hold the answers." I waited for Nick's glare to soften. It didn't but I pressed on. "I won't be intimidated by a name or reputation." I chose to interpret the silence from the other end of the table as agreement. "It's settled then. I'll call the Tagliannos tomorrow."

I stood, kissed Nick on the forehead, put our dirty plates in the sink, said I love you, and went to bed.

CHAPTER 20

Wednesday, October 30

Wednesday passed at a slugs pace. I was playing with two peach-faced lovebirds. They have fun personalities in a manageable size body, but require almost daily socialization to become tame. That's why I hand feed them everyday. They can live 10-15 years. This is far less than an African Grey; which can live past fifty years, but has a larger vocabulary. Lovebirds are not known to be great talkers, but they're a cuddly size. Most store bought animals can make great pets if you are educated, patient, and willing to make the time sacrifice. Discretionary placement of the right pet with the right owner is the most important part of my job.

Nick broke with tradition and showed up for lunch on Wednesday, bearing foot-long submarine sandwiches. "Hi, honey. It was a buy-one-get-one-half-off deal today. We can save the other sub for tomorrow." He set the sandwiches and two sodas on the table in the back room and pulled out plates and napkins. We said a quick prayer of thanks and dug in.

"I need to make a phone call and since Jessica's not here today would you mind watching the front counter for a minute?" I asked.

Nick nodded.

I picked up my plate and moved to my desk in the office next door. Grabbing a list of names and numbers I had written down earlier in the month I began dialing a local number, but not without some trepidation.

A sweet, soft voice answered, "Taglianno residence."

"Hello, Mrs. Taglianno? This is Morgan Langdon. I don't know if you remember our last meeting, but I know your husband does. I understand he wasn't too happy with my visit and I wanted to say I'm sorry for any problems I might have caused."

A gentle "Ahah" was the woman's only response.

I continued. "Anyhow, I'm writing an article for the *Newport Journal* about Emile Voorhees and I was hoping you might be able to talk your husband into granting me an interview."

The reply was polite but firm. "My husband and I didn't know Mr. Voorhees. I'm sure there's nothing we could tell you that would be of any help."

"Perhaps if you understood my motives," I said. "I've been interviewing a lot of people for my story and along the way I've run into quite a few innuendos regarding a possibly unsavory relationship between your husband and Mr. Voorhees. I thought perhaps before an unscrupulous reporter got the same information, your husband might like to give me his side of the story, set the record straight so to speak." I waited.

"I'm not sure I understand. What innuendos?" Gina Taglianno's tone was betraying her. She knew exactly what I meant, although Tony Taglianno might have attempted to hide the truth from his wife.

I pressed the point. "I'm sure you respect and love your husband as much as I do mine. I'm certain you wouldn't want to see his name dragged through the mud. That is why I am offering your husband an opportunity to talk with me. Employees of Emile Voorhees have given me the impression that there was bad blood between him and your husband because of some business dealings. What those were, I'm not sure, but if the police get more substantial information, they may exhume Voorhees's body and then your husband may be a suspect in a murder case. And with a name like Taglianno, nothing can shelter him from public scrutiny." I held my breath knowing I had taken some liberties.

"My husband won't be home until later this evening. I'm not making any promises except that I'll speak to him. Where can I get back to you?"

I rattled off my home phone and cell phone numbers. I thanked her for listening and guaranteed only the truth would be written in any article of mine.

As I hung up I heard voices coming from the counter out front. I pushed open the door and came face to face with Frank and Carol.

"Hi, Morgan." Carol waved a hand over the bags of cat food.

Nick, who was standing behind the counter, was discussing the latest facts about the case with Frank. I waved to Carol and said to Frank with a gleam in my eye, "What are the two of you doing?"

Although it was becoming clear the two of them no longer needed an excuse to spend time together, they still felt they needed to give others a reason. "Carol needed some cat food and I wanted to check on you and see how your investigation was going. We haven't talked for some time now," Frank said, without a trace of a speech impediment. He cleared his throat and looked in Carol's direction. "It just seemed more convenient for us to come in one vehicle."

I thought I detected a slight blush in Frank's cheeks. "The investigation is stalled, at least for now. Did Nick tell you about my visit with Barbara Voorhees and our trip to see Richard Taylor?"

He nodded.

"I don't believe Emile's wife had anything to do with his death, but Taylor I'm not so sure about. He doth protest too much, if you know what I mean."

"Is there anything I can do to help?" Frank asked with such authority I thought perhaps his mother had stayed in New York City after her last shopping expedition.

"Frank, what would your mother say?"

"Mother does not need to know everything I do." His cavalier smile belied his innermost feelings, I thought. His mother still intimidated him, but for now he was taking a step forward toward independence.

I thought for a moment about how Frank could assist. If nothing else I could use the investigation as another excuse to get Carol and him together again. "If you want to help, I have an idea. I couldn't get much out of the employees at the Brockton store. Perhaps you and Carol could take a jaunt up there and do some poking around. Maybe you can scare up something I couldn't."

By this time, Carol had brought her purchases to the counter. I rang up the total for one bag of premium kitten food, a few toy mice and some cat grass. She pulled out a charge card, handed it to me and said, "I haven't had this much excitement in my life since my cousin Gertrude's wedding. She married a trapeze artist who worked for Ringling Brothers and the couple held their ceremony thirty feet in the air. As they said their final vows they pushed off the stand and went swooshing back and forth on trapezes as the clowns threw fake water confetti over the guests."

"Is that for real?" I asked.

She placed a hand on Frank's bent elbow and said, "True story, really. Anyway, we'd love to spy for you, wouldn't we, Pookums?"

There was no mistaking the blush on Frank's cheeks this time. The pair left arm-in-arm, promising to get back to me as soon as they could.

"I need to get going too, honey. I'll see you after work," Nick said. He winked at me on his way out and made me promise I wouldn't get into any trouble, at least not before dinner.

CHAPTER 21

Thursday, October 31

Only a day had passed but I felt as if I had been waiting for a week. I needed to speak to the Taglliannos before I could make another move, but the ball was in their court. There wasn't much I could do if they didn't want to speak with me. The situation was different than with Voorhees, who had employees who were willing to rat on him. The Taglianno name, mob-related or not, was a powerful force and the last person I wanted to come face to face with was the head of the Taglianno family.

On this late Halloween afternoon, Nick and I relaxed in front of the television and a crackling fire, getting up occasionally to pass out candy to the trick-or-treaters who showed up at our door. Jessica was handling that responsibility in the shop.

The rush of candy-seekers was about over, and Nick's eyelids were drooping as he and Cooper lay on the couch in the snuggle pooch position—Nick with his back against the cushions and one arm dangling over Cooper's large black chest. I was curled up in my rocker, one leg hanging over the edge, as I flipped through the channels at breakneck speed.

I know they'll call. They have to. What choice do they have? My rocker was beating in time with my brain waves. "Honey," I said loud enough to wake Nick from his semi-slumber.

He and Cooper sat up at the same time with equally startled expressions. "What? What's wrong?"

"Nothing, except what a little phone call could cure. Do you think they'll call?" I was now pacing around the furniture. Cooper watched, his head following my movements like an owl pursuing a late-night snack.

"You need to take a lesson from the old Chinese proverb, 'She who cannot sit still will never gather moss.'" Nick bounced his eyebrows up and down, smiling.

"Chinese proverb? Right."

"Seriously, all that pacing and agonizing is not going to change things. Sit down and be patient. They'll call…eventually. Besides, we have other leads." He paused with a questioning look on his face. "Don't *we*?"

"I'm getting another cherry Coke. Do you want one, Mr. Wisenheimer?"

Four bottles of soda, two bags of buttery popcorn and a video later the phone rang. I told Nick to stay where he was; I wanted to answer. I cleared my throat and in a confident tone said, "Hello."

It's Mom. I mouthed the words as I rolled my eyes. "I'm sorry I haven't got back to you about dinner this weekend," I said. "We've got some things going on. I'm not sure we can make it this Saturday, maybe next week. Yes, I promise. Yes, I will tell him. Yes, Mom. I love you too. Okay. Call you. Bye."

I hung up annoyed, not from the conversation but from the disappointment that the caller hadn't been a Taglianno. "Mom said to tell you she'll see you next week for her cleaning appointment and if we don't have dinner with her and Dad by next weekend she's coming over here with lasagna." I sank into a chair and sighed with defeat. Just as I was deciding to put on my pajamas the phone rang again.

I jumped, my spine tingled and Cooper barked. "It's them," I said. "I know it is. Cooper senses these things and he's never wrong."

The phone kept ringing. “You’d better answer before they decide we’re not home,” Nick said, leaning into my shoulder so he could listen in on the conversation.

With hand trembling I raised the receiver to my ear. “Hello, Langdon’s.”

After a long moment of silence, a soft voice said, “Hello, this is Gina Taglianno. I am getting back to you about this weekend. My husband is willing to meet with you tomorrow night, for drinks, at the yacht club. Around seven.”

“That’s good,” I said, but before I could say more, she said, “We’ll see you then. Good-bye.”

I hung up. I turned to Cooper and patted my shoulders. “Let’s dance.” He stood on his back paws and placed his front ones on my shoulders. His one hundred fifteen pounds brought us face to face as we jigged around the carpet and I sang, “We’re going to the yacht club to solve this mystery. We’re going to the yacht club to nab us a killer.”

“What makes you so sure about that?” Nick asked, interrupting our celebration. “He may know nothing. He may tell you nothing. Then where will you be?” Nick pointed his thumb toward the floorboards.

I guided Cooper’s paws back to the ground. “Stop being such a pessimist and get your list of questions ready. Watson, we’re about to nail a killer . . . possibly.”

CHAPTER 22

Friday, November 1

Nick and I arrived at the yacht club at six thirty Friday evening. We wanted a chance to choose the table and set up the seating arrangement ahead of time. We decided to sit at the table we had the night of the Fall Fest Ball. It wasn't the best location, but most members preferred window seating, so a more remote table would afford us privacy in case the discussion got fiery.

"Let's go over our list one more time," I said. "One, we're going to ask him what the heated discussion was all about the night of the ball. Then depending on his answer we'll move onto number two. Was his threat meant to intimidate or was it meant as a promise? Three . . ."

Nick tapped me on the shoulder and pointed to the doorway. The Tagliannos were standing by the etched glass doors talking to the hostess. "They must have had the same idea as us. Get here early and be prepared. Guess we don't have time to go over number three," I whispered

We stood. Eyes met eyes in a cordial but restrained fashion. Nick motioned for the waiter who arrived, menus and pad in hand.

"We won't be needing those," Tony Taglianno said, handing the menus back to the waiter. "I'll have a Remy Martin on the rocks and she'll have an iced tea."

The waiter nodded and proceeded around the table. Nick ordered two glasses of the house Gewürztraminer for us.

We sat making restrained politically correct conversation: Gewürztraminer is one of our favorite wines. Hasn't this fall weather been lovely? Can you wait for the holiday season to begin? When the waiter arrived five minutes later with our drinks and I had something in my hands to fiddle with I said, "So tell me, Mr. Taglianno, what do you get out of Emile Voorhees's death?"

Everyone sat silent, aghast. I, as usual, wished my tongue were slower than my thought process. I cleared my throat and shifted my backside in the uncomfortable wooden chair. I hoped I hadn't ruined my chances of getting information by insinuating guilt.

"I'm sorry," I stammered. "Let me rephrase the question. It appeared to me the night of the Fall Fest Ball that you," I looked into the searing eyes of Tony Taglianno, "and Emile Voorhees had some issues. I overheard a fierce conversation the two of you were having. You were angry. It seems mighty convenient he died that very evening." This wasn't much better, but there was no turning back. I sat up straighter in my chair and grasped Nick's hand under the table for moral support.

Gina gave her husband a smile only a spouse would understand. It meant, I hoped, be calm and don't get your hackles up because the truth will win out.

He leaned over, squeezed his wife's arm and said, "Yes. You heard right. We had a difference of opinion. Emile Voorhees was a despicable, underhanded businessman and I can't say I'm sorry he's dead, but I didn't have anything to do with his death. Now let me ask you a couple of questions. Why is your paper interested in publishing an article? And have you checked with everyone involved with him? I'm quite certain there were others who would have liked to see him dead. Be that as it may, the last I heard, according to your paper, Voorhees died from suspicious causes, but that doesn't mean murder."

To tell the truth and nothing but the truth…I wondered if this was the right course to take. "The paper is interested because he was a prominent businessman with a successful business. I'm sure you can appreciate that. As to the latter, yes, I'm sure you're right. However, I can't tell you the specifics of anything. It's all still under investigation."

"Whatever the cause, the world is better off without him." Tony lifted his glass to a passing waiter to order another drink. "If he was murdered somebody did us all a favor."

I became indignant. "You may be a father someday. Would you want to teach your children that the truth is inconsequential? That allowing someone to go unpunished for a crime is fine as long as the victim is 'despicable' in your judgment?" I drew quotation marks in the air with my fingers. "What if someone murdered your father? Lots of people see him as contemptible. Would that justify his death?"

"All right, you made your point. I still don't understand what this has to do with me."

"Tell me what you and Voorhees were arguing about the night of the ball?" Here's where I paid close attention to his body language. Words could lie, but shifty eyes, sweaty palms and nervous knees could say much more.

This time Gina was the one who shifted in her seat, gazing down at the floor with pursed lips.

"If I hadn't already discussed this with my wife, she and I wouldn't be here this evening," Tony Taglianno said. "As it happens, though, our tenth anniversary was a couple of months ago and she needed to know the truth."

"The truth about what?" I leaned across the table, my eyes glued to his.

"I had handed down to me from my grandfather a piece of heirloom jewelry. It had been in the family for generations. My great-great-grandfather brought it over from

Italy at the turn of the century. It was a brooch with a six-carat cabochon emerald surrounded by sixteen carats of pink diamonds appraised at around forty thousand dollars. It was exquisite, but it had seen better days. Some of the settings were loose and I knew Beauty by Design had a good reputation for restoring antique jewelry, so naturally that's where I took it. After it was returned to me I placed it in my father's safe until I was ready to give it to my wife on our anniversary." He paused taking a sip of his second Remy.

"So what was the problem?" My impatience shone like the North Star on a clear night.

Tony set down his tumbler, wiping the side of his mouth with a knuckle. "I decided to have it reappraised by another store my father does business with. I wanted a second opinion. I was told all the jewels had been cleverly replaced with fakes."

My mind transfixed on the image of a dark-suited gentleman sitting in an empty warehouse. Propped in front of him was an old card table. He sat on a metal chair and opened a black case. People crowded around him but stayed silent as he pulled out his refractometer and polariscope, instruments used by gemologists. He peered at the brooch, made no sound, returned his instruments to their case, rose on arthritic knees and then pronounced solemnly, "It's a fake."

"Well, you can appreciate my anger, I'm sure," Tony Taglianno said, pulling me out of my reverie, "but Voorhees denied everything. I had a few conversations with him on the phone and I met with him once at his store. He was vehement, saying he didn't know what I was talking about." He looked at his wife who shifted uncomfortably in her chair. "Until the night of the ball, we didn't know he was a member of this club. When I saw him here, I confronted him again. Of course he denied everything and said my stones had been fakes all along."

Nick asked, "Didn't you have the brooch appraised before you went to Beauty by Design?" Nick's tone was scolding. I squeezed his knee under the table.

Taglianno, much to Nick's and my amazement, shook his head in frustration. "My grandfather had his own people appraise it years ago. There was no legitimate paperwork, just the handshake from someone my grandfather trusted. Now, except for the setting, it's worthless and Voorhees is dead. Don't you see that I'd be better off with him alive?"

"You may think that, but perhaps your father and grandfather don't. Could they have had him bumped off?" I crossed my arms and sat motionless.

Gina spoke up for the first time. "Don't be ridiculous. They weren't even here the night of the party. Besides, his father is the kindest, most giving man I know. Everyone assumes the worst about him. It's not fair."

It was obvious by the shifting of her eyes from me to Nick to the floor that she knew the truth about her father-in-law. She didn't want to admit that she'd married into a family of criminals.

I felt a momentary pang of guilt for making that assumption, but continued. "They may not have been here, but did your father know about the fakes?"

Tony looked at his wife, hesitated and said, "No. We couldn't bring ourselves to tell him the truth. There is no way my father could have had anything to do with Voorhees's death."

There it was—the body language I was looking for. That slight hesitation, the quick glance at each other. Someone wasn't admitting something, but what, I wasn't sure. Another push might make one of them slip. "It seems to me I remember the words restitution and perdition in the same sentence, Mr. Taglianno. Do I need to refresh your memory about the conversation on the back deck that night?"

"I'll remember the conversation for as long as I live. As I said before, I was angry. Haven't you ever said anything in anger before? It didn't mean anything other than what I said."

"And what was that?" Nick asked.

"That he would get what was coming to him. Either a day in court here on earth or a court at the feet of saints." He raised his glass to the heavens, stood and announced, "I think we've given you enough information for your story. And, as you promised, you'll be sure to get the facts straight about my family, correct?" He leaned over, helping his wife up from her chair as she pulled her jacket off the seat next to her. He held the garment for her as she slipped her arms in place. He turned to Nick and me. "We won't be discussing this again with anyone unless our attorney is present. Have a good evening." They left, never looking back.

"Do you think he was telling the truth or knew more than what he was letting on?" Nick waited for a response as I leaned back rubbing my belly. "Don't you feel well?"

"I can't think on an empty stomach. Let's order dinner." I raised my hand and waved to the waiter who moved from behind the bar and grabbed two menus.

Under his breath Nick announced, "Can't you ever do anything without thinking about food first?"

I shot Nick a reproving glance. I flipped through the dinner menu and then looked up to the waiter with a questioning grin? "Could I have a bowl of Onion soup, but could you put extra cheese on it, please?"

He bobbed his head and shrugged his shoulders. “Sure, no problem.” Then smiling straight-lipped he looked to Nick and said, “And what can I get for you?”

“I’ll have the dinner special, the panko crusted baked scrod with red potatoes.”

“Would you like extra panko on that?” He asked flipping his pad closed.

“No thanks, that will be all.”

The waiter nodded and marched off to the kitchen.

“The evening’s just beginning,” Nick said. “I’d hate to see his attitude by ten o’clock tonight.”

“He’s new, I think. If Art catches him acting like that he’ll get the boot.” I lifted up my knee and kicked Nick with my foot.

“I hope not too many patrons place a special order while he’s on duty. It may send him over the edge.” Nick impersonated old Mr. Flinch, flailing his fork in the air and saying in a crusty voice, “I’ll have absolutely no almonds on my trout almandine.”

I giggled. “I think you’ve missed your true calling, comedic impersonations.” I shook my head adding; “Some people are so odd about their special orders for a meal . . .” My eyes began glazing over as I stopped mid-sentence.

“Honey, hello, are you still in there?” Nick chuckled, probably because he had seen this happen so many times before.

“Yeah, I’m here. I was just remembering the night of the party and all the special meal requests.”

“Like Mr. Flinch’s?”

“Yes, and like Emile Voorhees’s.”

“I remember there were a few cock-eyed orders, but wasn’t Voorhees’s pretty reasonable?”

"That's not the point. It's that he *had* a special request that matters. Remember? Those individual table assignments had notations written in red on the cards so the kitchen staff would know to serve a special meal. Like Mr. Flinch was NA, no almonds. And Emile was NS, no salt." I drummed my fingers on the table and scrunched my forehead in thought.

"And your point is what?"

"That anyone who was here that evening would have known what plate was going to whom. I've always said that if this were foul play then the only logical conclusion would be poison. Think of all the suspects on our list. Most all were here, like Emile's wife. And Susan. And Tony Taglianno."

"Susan's dead and I can't believe it could have been her, unless we have two separate murders on our hands. And you yourself said you've ruled out Barbara Voorhees as a suspect." Nick said.

"Stop confusing the issue. I do believe Mrs. Voorhees is innocent and no, I don't think we have two murderers on our hands. However Taglianno was here and we don't personally know all the kitchen employees. Maybe Tony's father had some hired help for the evening."

"I think Art would have questioned a waiter he didn't hire."

"But things were so hectic that night, I'm not sure Art would have noticed a new face. What if a stranger slipped in for a moment in a white waiter's outfit?"

"That's possible, I guess, but I'm wondering about Richard Taylor. He's not a member but maybe he's a suspect."

"True enough. Emile had just left work. Some poisons take some time to kick in. Maybe he was poisoned earlier in the afternoon in a cup of coffee. With a little maneuvering Taylor or any of his employees would have easy access to the cache of special coffee blends Voorhees kept in his office?

"In that case, anyone could have done it, so we're back to square one." Nick lifted both hands in the air motioning as if he were throwing in the towel. "I would like to know how you became such an expert on poisoning anyway."

"The Internet."

"Remind me to unsubscribe. You and Google are a frightening combination." Nick rolled his eyes.

I stuck out my tongue in self-defense as our dinners arrived. Art Leadbetter delivered our meals in person, tray in hand and his salt-and-pepper mustache well groomed.

"You're the jack-of-all-trades around here. Don't tell me you're short on waiters again," I said.

"No. Todd, your waiter, is new and a bit green. He needs some more training in his people skills. He's in the back being reprimanded by my head waiter." Art set our plates carefully before us in proper English-butler fashion. "If you don't mind my asking, what do the two of you have in common with Tony Taglianno? He doesn't seem the sort you'd be hanging around."

Nick answered. "Nothing. And you're right."

I squeezed Nick's knee under the table again. "I'm doing an article for the *Journal* about Emile Voorhees's life and his business. Taglianno and his wife are among the people I've interviewed. I like to be thorough." I didn't want to add any more details. Not everyone was privy to the notion that Emile's death might have been murder. It was bad enough people knew his death was dubious at best. Perhaps Susan's death wasn't accidental either. I wanted to keep those ideas to myself for now.

"Oh, I see. Well, I'd be careful if I were you. I'm sure you've heard about his family. I wouldn't want to get on their bad side. Might not be good for your health." He filled our water glasses and asked if we needed anything else.

"Actually, if you have a second I wouldn't mind asking you a few questions since you once lived in Boston." I said.

"Questions about what?" Art's eyes narrowed.

"I meant perhaps you saw the Beauty by Design ads and commercials more than we did here in Harbor View. I'm trying to cover all the bases on his life and business. I'm looking for anyone with an opinion, if you'd like to share yours."

He stood straighter, looking almost stunned for an instant. "I don't think I could add anything worthwhile. Owning my own business I didn't watch TV much. I didn't have time to read the papers and my wife and daughter were never interested in wearing that type of jewelry. I knew of the business by name, but not reputation. If you'll excuse me, I have to get back to the kitchen." He gave a polite bow of the head and left.

I guessed Art didn't care for Emile any more than anyone else did. We finished our meal in quiet contemplation, both Nick and I wondering what the next move should be. Leaving, we walked arm-in-arm across the parking lot; the only sounds were those of our footsteps on the gravel and the unspoken words on our mind.

CHAPTER 23

Saturday, November 2

An uneasy quiet settled over our kitchen Saturday morning. Nick had showered and was operating in robot mode, going through the past few days' mail at the kitchen table. Cooper lay stretched on the pine floor with one of his favorite teddy bears nestled between his paws. I stood near the sink, watching cartoons on our countertop TV.

"What do you want to do today?" Nick asked. He was sorting the mail into three piles: the bill pile, the throwaway pile and the read-it-later pile. "Jessica is running the shop today, right?"

He waited for a response.

I kept staring at the television.

Cooper raised his head. His eyelids were half-open. When he saw nothing of importance he lay back down, covering the stuffed toy with his head.

Nick spoke again, "Morgan, speak to me. What's going on in that pretty little head of yours?"

I didn't turn away from the screen. "I love SpongeBob," I said.

Nick rose and walked over to me. Placing his arm around my shoulder, "Maybe you should sit down, honey. This has been a tough few weeks. The stress must be getting the better of you." He tried moving me over to a chair, but I stopped him mid-step.

"I know what we're going to do today after our volunteer work. We're going to Finnigan's Bar and Grill. A little late lunch, a little loose lip may equal a lot of information. I've got to shower." I grabbed my orange juice and turned toward the bathroom.

Cooper raised his head again and moaned. He pushed himself up onto all fours, walked over to Nick and looked up into his face. He received a soft pat on the head. "I think your mom needs a long cruise to some faraway island. In the meantime, I suppose we'll have to humor her." The giant ball of brown fur lowered his front legs to the ground stretching his backside to the ceiling and moaned.

A couple of hours later Nick and I entered the dimly lit restaurant. The soft glow of fake gaslight glimmered on the polished wooden tabletops. The lunch hour was busy. Patrons were buzzing in and out. Waiters and waitresses were hovering over them like bees on blossoms. There would be a twenty-minute wait. The hostess suggested we sit at the bar. That suited me just fine. That's where I wanted to be—right where the trouble began the last time I was here.

We grabbed two stools smack in the middle. Everyone must have been in the kitchen because no one greeted us.

"What if Mr. Finnigan or his grandson isn't working today, what should we do?" Nick asked.

"Waitresses, waiters. They'll talk. They see and know everything that goes on, especially if they've been here long enough. Trust me. We'll get some answers before we leave," I said.

I squirmed and fidgeted on my barstool until I saw Patrick Finnigan. He turned the corner from the kitchen and came around facing the bar, singing along with the Irish tune that was playing over the speaker system. "Oh, I woke me up this morning and I heard a joyful song, from the throats of happy Irishmen, a hundred thousand strong."

He strolled down the bar waving to everyone. When he got to me he stopped short. "I never forget a face. Hello again, lassie. Wasn't sure you'd be back."

"Why's that?" I asked.

"One of my waitresses told me my grandson wasn't very polite to you after I left. I apologize. His mother, my daughter Maggie, wanted me to help keep him on the straight and narrow. Giving him a job here was her idea. I didn't much cotton to the prospects. Hard manual labor on a fishing boat would have done him better, but his mother said she'd worry too much." He waved to a customer letting him know he'd be right over. "Doesn't much matter now though. He's doing time for dealing drugs." He shook his head in dismay and left to take an order.

"Why doesn't that surprise me?" I said to Nick over the clamor of the crowd. "I knew he was hiding something when I asked him about Emile and Captain Omnipotence." I tried remembering the exact conversation we had. "It wasn't the words the grandson used as much as it was his tone and attitude."

"That doesn't mean he knew Emile," Nick said.

"If he didn't know anything then why would he have been so defensive about my asking? I can't find any logical explanation other than that he knew more than he wanted to let on, probably because divulging anything could get him into trouble. Obviously that's true since he's in jail now. Can't you see the connection?" I looked at Nick, raising my eyebrows.

"You're saying Emile was either buying or selling drugs just as you suspected."

I touched my nose with my index finger. "You got it, and maybe this Captain person was his middleman, and what if Emile owed him money? How many times do we hear on the news about someone getting shot over a drug deal gone bad?"

"I won't argue that point, but Emile wasn't shot. According to you he was poisoned. That doesn't sound like some bad-ass drug dealer's modus operandi, does it?"

"Yeah, you've got a point. But maybe these are more sophisticated drug dealers, not just the run-of-the-mill, back-alley kind. Besides, they could have done the stabbing thinking they killed him." I tried to believe my assessment, but I had to admit to myself that Nick was probably right. A leather-coated, chain-smoking biker didn't fit the stereotypical killer who bludgeoned or poisoned for revenge or payoff. He was the type of guy who would meet you in a back alley and shoot you dead and run, not worrying about DNA or trace evidence. Before I had a chance to contemplate any further, Patrick returned, his Irish brogue and elfish smile intact.

He glanced at Nick with a dubious expression and asked, "Is he with you?"

I smiled and apologized for not making proper introductions. "I'm sorry, yes. This is my husband, Nick. He decided to come along today."

Nick reached out his hand and shook the thick hairy fingers of Patrick Finnigan. "You have a nice place and a good Irish singing voice. We heard your rendition of 'It's a Great Day for the Irish.'"

"You're familiar with the song? You must have a wee bit of Irish in you." He winked his eye at Nick.

"Not me. What I do have is a father-in-law who's Irish and thinks his singing voice is a gift from the fairies." He leaned in, cupping his hand to his cheek. "He sounds more like a wailing banshee to me."

I slapped him across the arm. He feigned a wince. "Don't mind him. He's just jealous," I said. "His vibrato sounds like a hairy woodpecker on a hollow tree." I sneered in Nick's direction.

"I didn't mean to start a family feud. Can I get you two anything to eat?"

We ordered fish and Diet Coke. Then before Patrick could get away I tried my Columbo shtick. "Mr. Finnigan, just one more thing." I looked around at the eddying crowd of hungry patrons. "Actually I was hoping to take a minute of your time," I stammered, knowing how he might respond to any mention of Emile Voorhees, "for a few questions."

"Sure, lass. I feel required to oblige after the way my grandson treated you. Can you wait for thirty minutes or so until I can get someone to fill in for me?"

We shook our heads like synchronized swimmers to show we would be glad to wait.

Our food order was plopped in front of us like slop in a trough. At these busy hours getting the orders right and delivered was more important than proper serving etiquette. As usual I finished my food before Nick. He believed in chewing and savoring every bite; my objective was instant gratification of the taste buds. While we were slurping the last of our sodas I began to feel a headache. I pulled two aspirin from my purse, asked for a refill on my drink and swallowed the pills, praying the pain would abate.

"I think the stress of interrogation is getting to me." I leaned my head against Nick's shoulder, checking my watch. It had been fifty minutes since Patrick had promised to give us some time. I was beginning to wonder if we shouldn't have made an appointment instead of just showing up on the sly. As if on cue, Finnigan came bounding through the kitchen door.

"I see you two are finished eating. Let's go back to my office. My hearing's not so good in a crowded space anymore." He motioned for us to make our way around the bar. He walked us past the grill and gas burners, around a couple of stacked wooden crates filled with produce and down a back hall. The door to his office was open. I entered, feeling glad for the absence of noise and the abundance of space. Fresh air came streaming through a partially opened window to my left. I breathed in deep like a prisoner getting his first feel of freedom.

Patrick apologized for the mess as he slid piles of junk off the chairs and onto the floor. He pointed down at the brown Naugahyde upholstery. "Have a seat. Now what's this all about? You said you had questions?" He walked to his desk, picked up a carved pipe and lit up, going over to stand near the window. "I hope you don't mind the pipe, but it's my way of relaxing."

Cigarette smoke annoyed me, but pipe smoke reminded me of my grandfather. The smell of pipe tobacco was aromatic, with its Old World mix of spices and herbs. It brought back memories of dancing with my papa. My tiny feet would straddle his as we danced on the cushiony grass of our backyard. I imagined myself a winged nymph as he lifted me into the air and swung me around.

"I love pipes. Is that made from meerschaum?"

"Now how would you know about meerschaum?" He exhaled rings of smoke that danced in the breeze from the window.

I felt obliged to explain. "My grandfather. He was Irish and owned a meerschaum pipe too. He told me meerschaum is a mineral mined in Turkey. It is used to make pipes because it's very permeable. I see yours is quite brown. You must use it a lot. Don't they start out white?" I usually knew at least one trivial fact about everything, often to Nick's annoyance.

"That's one smart lassie you have there," Finnigan said to Nick. He pointed at me with his pipe. "Enough about pipes. How can I help you?"

In my experience, people fall into two categories when they are interviewed. Some people are like parrots. They love to hear their own voices. They love seeing their names in print. Then there are the clams. They are the silent types who are afraid to say anything for fear something will be used against them in court. Which type is Patrick Finnigan I wondered?

"I'm an investigative reporter for the *Newport Journal.* I'm doing a piece on Emile Voorhees. You mentioned last time I was here that he used to frequent your restaurant." I postured reporter doggedness.

Patrick nodded his head. He took a long drag from his pipe and leaned into the wall. "What are you investigating?"

"His life in general, his acquaintances, his business practices? Things like that." I wasn't sure how specific I should be at this juncture.

"Sounds to me like you're on a fishing expedition. What are you fishing for?"

I formulated at that moment a third category of interviewee: those who answer a question with a question. "Mr. Finnigan, the truth is…" I stood up and walked into his comfort zone "…we believe Emile Voorhees was murdered." I took a moment to explain the circumstances and the need for discretion. "We don't have any proof. That's why I'm here. You might know something that could give us a clue. Even a seemingly insignificant fact could lead to the truth. Voorhees came here often; you must have seen and heard things. I need you to share whatever you know." My eyes pleaded for a response.

He patted me on the shoulder, walked to his desk and knocked the ashes from his pipe into a large ashtray. "I'm not one to spread rumors. As long as customers come in, act polite and pay their bill, I don't much care what else they do or say." He paused, sitting down in a high-back swing chair. "Emile Voorhees was always dapper, but there was something sinister about him. He never failed to reserve the back booth." He looked at me. "I showed you the one." I nodded, remembering the moment. "I knew he was buying drugs." Then seeing my eyes widen he added, "No, no, I can't prove a thing. He would meet on a regular basis with this shady character in a black leather jacket. The guy wore that thing all year round even in the heat of summer. I think he thought it made him look intimidating."

"I'm pretty sure I met that guy in your parking lot the first night I was here. He can be a bit intimidating," I said.

"He didn't hurt you, did he?" Finnigan looked concerned.

"No, I was fine. I'm sorry, go on."

"My grandson, as you know, was arrested for cocaine possession a couple of days after you were here. He's not talking to the police, but I did. I pointed out the guy in the leather jacket, but so far they haven't picked him up or charged him with anything as far as I know." Patrick slapped the desk with his hand. "Every sin gets punished. He'll get his sometime, somehow. Anyway, Voorhees used to meet women here too. There were two or three he saw often. I'm certain there was more to those meetings than met the eye."

"How can you be so sure? Maybe they were business meetings or friends." I knew better, but I wanted Finnigan's read.

"A few years back he and his wife were on a local TV broadcast discussing the opening of a new store. The women I saw him with weren't his wife. Besides, he and these women would hold hands and order wine and look at each other the way lovers do. Then they would leave the bar arm-in-arm." Patrick blushed. It was obvious he wasn't comfortable talking about a stranger's sex life.

"Were there ever any heated discussions? Did you ever get a name or can you describe any of the women to us?"

"No to the arguments. He was always Mr. Suave with the women. There were a few conversations with some men I thought might get out of control, but nothing ever came of them. Who the women were, I have no idea. What they looked like, well, there was so many it's too hard for this old brain to remember. Although this past year or so there were two women he saw quite often. Let me think a minute." He stopped, scratching his head. "They were both very pretty. One was taller with dark-brown medium-length hair. I'm not so good with ages. Everybody looks young to someone my age. But if I had to take a guess, I'd say about thirty-five, give or take. She was one of those self-assured types—knew what she wanted and how to get it. Then there was a pretty blonde, not nearly as tall as the other one. He saw her regularly for about a year or so. She seemed too young and vulnerable for someone his age, but maybe that's acceptable nowadays. Those were the two I saw the most of. He saw others, though. As to the men, there were more than I could count. One I think was his partner; the other was the fellow in the leather jacket, like I said. I haven't seen him around much since my grandson was arrested. Good riddance to him. I hope he never returns. I'm not certain how any of this is going to help you."

I pondered his words for a moment. I wasn't sure myself if anything he had told me was important. The tall brunette was probably Susan Fairfield and she wouldn't be talking. The other woman I hadn't a clue. Two things seemed more certain: Voorhees was either buying or selling drugs and the man in the leather jacket was too. Other than that I had hit another impasse.

I picked up my purse from the floor, stood and thanked Finnigan for his time. "You have helped. I appreciate your taking time out of your busy schedule. When I get the article done, I'll send you a copy." I reached out to shake his hand.

We received a Finnigan Irish blessing on the way out the door, "May the road be down hill all the way to your front door."

We walked to the car in silence. Nick said nothing; I think he felt the dead end as keenly as I did. I was contemplating a long hot bath when we got home as my cell phone rang.

I scrambled, trying to locate the sound. I found the phone in the pocket of my jacket and answered the call, seconds before the voice mail would have kicked in. The call was from Frank and Carol. They had just returned to Carol's house in Harbor View.

Frank's pride and confidence beamed through in his voice. I decided his undercover work with a pretty woman at his side was good medicine, because he said without a single mispronounced word, "I think we know who killed Emile Voorhees."

CHAPTER 24

Nick and I wanted to hear the story firsthand so we hung up, arranging for all four of us to meet at our home. It took us fifteen minutes less than normal to return to Harbor View because we drove at breakneck speed. Frank and Carol were waiting. Nick unlocked the door. Cooper bounded into the yard and lifted his leg on the first fence rail. I opened a bottle of wine to celebrate with a toast. The excitement was premature. When we sat down at the kitchen table Frank began fidgeting with his keys. Carol placed a hand over his to quiet his nervous fingers.

"Why don't you two start at the beginning?" I said. "Last I knew you were going to the Brockton store. What did you learn there that makes you think you know Emile's killer?"

Carol spoke first. "We may have spoken out of turn," she said, eyes downcast.

"It's not Carol's fault. I was overeager and wanted to be the one who solved this *cwime*. I may have taken more *wibewty* than I should have in saying we know exactly who the killer is." Frank's speech impediment was growing in direct proportion to his anxiety.

"No, no. It's just as much my fault. I was certain we had the answer, but now I'm not so sure. It was both of us," Carol said.

Frank smiled gratefully at Carol.

"Enough already, you two. Good grief, just give it to me straight. What did you find out?" I dribbled some wine onto the front of my blouse.

"We'll start at the beginning," Carol said. "You wanted us to see if we could find out anything more from the employees at the Brockton store. Frank and I went there this afternoon. We pretended to be looking for an engagement ring." Judging from the looks they exchanged, their ruse might not have been far from the truth. "We spoke to a gentleman by the name of Larry Lindbeck who was quite cooperative. He didn't seem to mind delving into personal matters. You would have been so proud of our questioning techniques."

"I'm sure I will be." Nick elbowed me. I jumped in my seat. "Sorry. Please, continue."

"It seems all the men and women who worked for Beauty by Design for more than a year were given a gift: the men a tie clasp, the women a necklace," Frank said, his speech impediment absent and his confidence apparently returning.

"I know that already, guys. How's that connected to the murderer?"

"According to Larry there was more than one design, depending on who the recipient was," said Carol.

I was finally beginning to think their trip had been worthwhile. This information could be helpful after all.

"All the men's tie clasps were made of mother of pearl set inside a ring of sterling silver. The design was very nice. Larry was wearing his," Frank said.

Carol added, "The women were given a similar design that looked like the tie clasp, with the same mother of pearl except in necklace form. But the women in his life who were special, you know affair material, received a heart design with a marquis diamond in the middle. Interesting, isn't it?"

"Very," Nick and I chimed in unison.

"But what's more interesting," Frank said, "is that when Voorhees decided a woman wasn't special anymore—I'm bored…I'm moving on—he asked for the necklace back, and if the woman worked for him, he gave her the mother of pearl design in its place. Can you believe this guy?"

I was astonished. How could he be so cold and unfeeling?

"There was one particular girl the week before Emile died," Carol continued. "She got the heave ho, so to speak, after closing one night. I guess Emile thought all the employees had gone home, but Larry was in the back. After telling her he was bored and was moving on, she told him directly that she was not giving her necklace back and he could take the other one and put it where the sun doesn't shine. According to Larry she left screaming and kicking, swearing her revenge. Larry is positive she used the words, 'I'm going to kill you so you can't do this to anyone else ever again.'"

"That sounds very encouraging. Did you happen to get a name?"

Frank and Carol high-fived each other before Carol pulled from her purse an old shopping list with the name Roxanne Lyle written on it in lipstick. She shrugged. "It was all I had to write with at the time. Anyway Larry says she is a tall good-looking redhead. And get this. She still works there."

"Something about this, the necklace, the red hair, it's all ringing a bell," I said.

Cooper rose and walked to my side, nudging my hand with his cold nose. I petted his shiny brown fur and jiggled his heart-shaped collar charm. It bore our address and phone number and it sparkled in the kitchen light. "Yes, I know who she is. I saw the necklace on her. I spoke to her myself when I was in Brockton. There was an air of evasiveness about her."

Before I could stand up Nick beat me to it and pushed down on my shoulder. "Before Morgan jumps in the car and runs off to goodness knows where, could I ask a few questions? Frank, do you happen to know the names of the other women who acquired and then lost this same necklace?" he asked

"Not right now, but I'm sure I could get them."

"Then how do we know the other women didn't have the same reaction and Larry just wasn't around to hear their sentiments? What if they all reacted the same way? And this Roxanne still had her necklace, maybe others kept theirs too," Nick continued. "We've all said things we don't mean literally. Remember, Morgan, when you told me you wished my mother would drive off the end of the pier and float away? You didn't mean that."

"Yes, I did."

Nick cupped my mouth with his hand. "Don't you see we can't run into one of Voorhees's stores and accuse someone of murder without any evidence? Let's be logical about this." Nick took a deep breath. "I have two suggestions. One, we find out the names of the other women he wooed into thinking they were his one and only until the big break-up. Maybe they had the same idea as Roxanne. And second, let's find out if Roxanne has an alibi."

Frank and Carol nodded in agreement.

Nick had taken his hand away and looked down at me. I was busy chewing on the side of my cheek and staring out the window. He knocked his knuckles against my head. "Hellloooow. Anyone in there?"

"What? Oh yeah, that makes sense." I moved around the table cleaning up the glasses and the now empty bottle. There was still something nagging at the back of my brain. The necklaces…Barbara Voorhees…the Tagliannos…maybe I had been wrong about everyone and everything. I had been so certain of their guilt at one point in time, only to change my mind later. Would Roxanne Lyle be any different? I felt a wave of failure sweeping over me.

"I think we should go straight back to Beauty by Design and get names and addresses for all those women," Carol declared.

Frank pounded his fist on the table and swore he would do anything for the cause of justice, no matter what his mother thought.

"How about you two go and find out what Roxanne was up to the night of the party and who else may have received one of those special necklaces," I said. "Now remember, be as discreet as possible. I've got some things I need to think about." I kissed them both on their cheeks and admonished them to be careful. The weather forecast said another storm was headed our way.

Frank and Carol left in Carol's car. Watching them drive away I realized at least one good thing had come from all of this. Two lonely people found each other and became friends.

Nick and I went out into the backyard and took turns throwing a Frisbee to Cooper until he dropped the disk from his mouth. That was his way of saying "I've had enough doggie Olympics for one night." Back inside the kitchen I heard the phone ring. I moved to answer, rubbing my eyes. I was beginning to feel major fatigue and frustration. Nick grabbed the phone before I could get to it.

"Hello. Yes, Mrs. Chesney. Yes, not a problem. I can be there in about twenty minutes." He hung up the receiver and turned to me. I had seen that look a hundred times before. "It's an emergency. An older patient of ours had a minor traffic accident and lost some teeth. I'm not sure how long I'll be."

"Do you need my help?" I asked as I stifled a yawn.

Normally Nick would have requested an extra pair of hands to grab instruments, but he could see I was wiped out.

"No, I'll be fine. My prescription for you while I'm gone is bunny slippers, hot cocoa and a video. I'll be home as soon as I can. Love you."

After he left I started for the bedroom, feeling apathetic about any further hunting for evidence. I found my slippers lying under one of my many dog-embroidered bathrobes. I slipped them on and made my way to the family room where I had left my laptop. Something was nagging at me, but I couldn't figure out what. I plopped down in front of the computer and idly hit the "on" button. My stomach growled. The dinner hour had come and gone. With all the excitement of Frank and Carol's report, we had eaten nothing. Thank goodness for leftovers and a Diet Coke. That would do the trick.

I licked the cheese residue from my fingers and looked over some notes I had made about suspects, clues and unanswered questions. It seemed everything was a dead end unless by some miracle I could locate a poison that would mimic death by heart attack or the toxicologist found something.

I had to face facts. Without further evidence, no judge would reopen this case without specifics. I leaned over my laptop, tangled my fingers in my hair and reviewed the suspects.

First there was Barbara Voorhees. It seemed she would have a perfect motive: revenge. How many affairs could one husband have without eliciting his wife's scorn and hatred? She had means too, at least in the matter of proximity to the deceased. I wanted to believe she was innocent, though, if only for Cocoa's sake.

Then there were the Tagliannos. There were so many of them, which one could I pick? It could have been the son; it could have just as easily been the father or a hired professional. Although, as Nick insisted, would a hit man really use poison, and why the knife postmortem?

Access to the building that night was simple: two back doors that weren't locked on a night of drinking and dancing. Anyone could have committed the "double" murder and in my mind that's what it was. There was any number of people who wanted Voorhees dead. Between partners, gambling creditors, drug dealers and old lovers the list seemed endless. I was trying to rule out the obvious, but my head started swimming and they all seemed plausible.

"Morgan, Morgan. Think logically. Be systematic. Organize your thought process," I said out loud. A jolt of adrenaline raced through me as Cooper barked in my ear. My brain snapped to attention as I took another bite of cold cheese and crackers. "Good grief, this case really is sending me over the edge. I bet I've gained five pounds in stress eating." Eyeing the last bit of food, I decided sharing was the thing to do, so I laid my plate on the floor. Cooper was more than glad to clean up the leftovers.

I touched my laptop mouse to wake up my system. If I didn't come up with something to substantiate my hunches, Sherman would soon be stamping both the Fairfield and the Voorhees files CASE CLOSED.

I clicked an icon on my desktop to open a folder containing the pictures I had taken of Emile's calendar. I remembered how little of it had made sense to me at first. Since then some of it had become clearer. I now understood why he went to Finnigan's so often—if not for drugs then for women. But some of the calendar entries were still a puzzle. Captain Omnipotence, I felt certain, had something to do with the leather-jacketed thug who accosted me, which meant it had something to do with drugs, but why the mystifying name? If Voorhees didn't want anyone to know what he was up to, why put such entries on his calendar at all? Perhaps he simply liked the coded cloak-and-dagger illusion of it all, as his wife had implied. Perhaps he simply thought rearranging words was clever. I repeated the word in my head: *rearranging…rearranging.*

I knew there was some other term for that. A word that meant transposing letters and making new words from them. Anamail? Gramma something? I tilted my head to the left and slapped my right ear as if I were trying to clear some seawater from the canal.

Anagram. That's it. I bet he used anagrams. Why hadn't I thought of this sooner? With my untimely, yet astute deduction, I hoped to unravel some of Emile's calendar. By doing so I might either add some names to the list of suspects or better yet, cross some off.

I entered C-A-P-T-A-I-N O-M-N-I-P-O-T-E-N-C-E in forty-eight-point type and then stared at the screen. The possibilities seemed endless. Short one-syllable words were easy. I could already see *I, am, in, mean, not, nice.* I began a list of words on one side of my document. After spending a few more minutes I started getting the hang if it and could pull out longer words like *patience, impotent,* and *poetic*. Not words Emile Voorhees was likely to use. This was getting me nowhere. It could take me forever to come up with a complete list of words and phrases. I clicked onto the Web. Maybe I could find an Internet anagram site. It was worth a try because I was tired and I could work until morning and still come up with nothing more than *one impotent poet*. I knew that couldn't possibly be right.

I searched and found a site offering a free trail. The user could enter as many as five phrases free of charge. The service would then unscramble the words into all the possibilities. The program listed the results categorically according to probabilities. A combination that had the qualities of a good sensible anagram would get a high percentage rating. One that didn't make much sense would get a lower score.

I typed "Captain Omnipotence" and pushed "search." I watched the screen as the program sorted the letters at breakneck speed. It didn't take long for the computer to come up with a huge list of possibilities. But the first words on the list earned a score of ninety-two percent: "Cocaine Appointment." Of course! That made perfect sense! Patrick Finnigan had suspected that drug deals were being made in his back booth. The captain was no captain at all, merely a reminder to buy an illegal drug.

I hoped Emile would stay true to form and that every nonsensical listing would be an anagram. I tried the next phrase on my list to test my theory: Ta! Sex Due. That was the listing Barbara was certain meant Emile had an appointment with his female tax accountant. Again I entered the words and watched as the screen scrolled through all the plausible entries. Sure enough the first entry at eighty-two percent said "due taxes!" Voorhees had been sneaky enough to devise anagrams to dissuade wondering, curious eyes from tracking his calendar entries, but once I had figured out his system, I had little doubt what he had been up to.

I entered a couple of other obscure phrases into the computer, such as "And in is a coin." The program spewed out less meaningful words. It took awhile for me to weed through the list of possible meanings, but two words looked probable: Indian and casino. They made sense. There was a casino owned by the Pequot Indians in Connecticut, plus I remembered one of the employees making mention of Voorhees's gambling problem. The decoding process was going well, not that any of this information was solving the mystery of who had killed Emile Voorhees.

I was left with one last free try. Any more and I would have to pay for the privilege of using the program. I searched through my list, contemplating which phrase looked the most promising. I wished Nick were here to bounce things off. There was "It a Gang," "Eh Excel New Jag" and a handful more that had potential. I finally decided on "The Celebrated Learn" because I liked the cadence. That was at least as good a reason as any to choose it. I typed in the letters, hit search and waited as a cold rain began to fall.

CHAPTER 25

The list of anagrams appeared on my screen, but nothing made sense. I filed through the columns and rows, word by word, my eyes narrowing with weariness. None of the possibilities rang any bells, not even a tiny jingle. I decided my brain was fried. I closed my programs, shut off the computer and sat back to finish the last few sips of my soda.

Stretching my legs I watched bleary eyed as the rain began to patter against my front window just as it had the fatal night of the ball. I let my mind wander back to that evening to see if there was anything I could have missed—a word, a gesture anything that would have spelled M-U-R-D-E-R-E-R. I couldn't help but think there was something I had overlooked, something obvious.

Sure, I had heard arguments and threats, but perhaps this crime—if there was one—was spun from finer threads. It had to be. The obvious wasn't working. Susan had threatened Voorhees, but she was dead. Barbara didn't have a real motive; even revenge seemed unlikely because she had already filed for divorce. Whatever love she had felt for her husband was long gone. And as to the leather-jacketed Captain Omnipotence, I figured too many of his brain cells had burned up a long time ago. He was a seller and an intimidator no doubt, but a murderer by poison? I doubted it. So who is left?

The Tagliannos. I couldn't figure them out. Tony seemed legitimate enough, but who knows how deep family bonds can go. I recalled how Nick and I had danced around the ballroom, then stopped and overheard the argument between Emile and Tony. If only I could have seen what was to come. I remembered the road being flooded and the commodore entreating everyone to stay at the yacht club until the storm blew over. Then there was the moment when Emile was on the dance floor with Barbara. He had gazed over his wife's shoulder, teetering, looking like someone who had substantial damages to compensate, a bill he would never be able to pay in full measure.

In my mind's eye I turned to gaze in the direction Emile would have been looking. Who was standing there? Who could have caused such a look of distress on his face? I strained to recapture that microsecond of information.

Big band music swelled in my head as the remembered scene came into focus. The Tagliannos sat hand-in-hand at their table. Beyond them Susan stood by the hallway, staring stone-faced with a drink in her hand. To her left—alone at the end of the bar—stood a figure, a tiny glimmering object dangling from one hand. The shiny object swayed like a pendulum. Why hadn't I remembered that? I had seen such an object before, one on a redheaded jewelry store clerk, but there were others like it.

Could it possibly be? I grabbed my napkin, snatched a stump of pencil from a drawer in the end table, and wrote T-H-E C-E-L-E-B-R-A-T-E-D L-E-A-R-N and I-T-A-G-A-N-G. I began rearranging the letters. Then I turned on my computer, opened my Google search engine and looked up some year-old obituaries. I was not surprised at what I found.

I made four phone calls, the first being to Nick. His phone rang six times before his recorded voice came on. "Hi. You've reached Nick Langdon, but I'm not able to take your call. Leave me a message and I'll get back to you as soon as I can." I waited for the recording to finish while I twirled my finger for it to hurry up. "To leave your call back number-press five. At the tone leave your message. When you have finished recording you may press one for more options." Beep.

"Nick, I sure hope this isn't the time you decide not to check your cell phone for messages. I'm going to the yacht club. It's ten forty-five. I know who the real killer is and why. Get your butt over there ASAP. Yes, I know what you're thinking. This is not some wild goose chase, I hope. Just do it! Love you. Bye."

I couldn't imagine his emergency appointment would have taken this long. I decided to leave a note on the refrigerator just in case. I made three more phone calls, and left three more messages, one of them being to Mark Sherman.

I couldn't imagine what was up with no one answering. Of all the times for everyone to be busy, this had to be it.

As I drove to the yacht club I wondered why I hadn't figured things out earlier. Perhaps I hadn't wanted to. Maybe that's why I had compiled lists of gamblers and drug addicts and Mafia men, because the obvious, at least in one case, was far too painful to imagine. All the clues pointed in one direction though; the conclusion was inescapable.

The rain was falling in sheets as I jumped from my car in the yacht club parking lot, looking around for other vehicles. The lights were dim inside the club. I struggled to get the right key into the lock and opened the door. I stepped inside, closing the door behind me, but leaving it unlocked should Nick or Mark Sherman get my message and follow me. Maybe I should have waited for Nick, I thought as I tiptoed down the hall, feeling as if eyes were following me. I laid my purse and cell phone on the hostess's table at the dining room entrance.

"Morgan, I see you're here. I got your message."

I swung around, caught off guard by Art Leadbetter, who had slipped through the kitchen door unnoticed. I stepped back closer toward the table.

"You were the second person I called," I said, keeping my tone even.

"You must have something you'd like to discuss with me. How about we go over to the bar. I'll pour you a drink. On me."

I was reluctant. A drink might cloud my judgment or worsen my sense of balance. I was also disinclined to follow him, but I went to the bar anyway, not wanting to create a mood of distrust. Not yet, at least. Art moved to the back of the bar, opened a small refrigerator and extracted from it an already opened bottle of wine. He poured two glasses carrying them around to the front of the bar before sitting down and placing one in front of me.

He raised his glass and said, "To a person I would have been proud to call my daughter." Then he gulped down the entire glass.

I was taken aback. For once in my life I was speechless. I raised my glass to him and forced a sorrowful smile before taking a small sip. I set the glass down and placed the napkin with the rearranged letters in front of him. I explained where I had seen this written and that it was an anagram. Art could see for himself that "The Celebrated Learn" translated into Charlene Leadbetter. "Her Clean" could be rearranged into Charlene.

"Art, tell me the truth about your daughter. She didn't die in a car accident with your wife, did she?"

His eyes welled with tears. "She was always such a sensitive child. Do you know the saying, 'She wouldn't hurt a fly'?"

I nodded.

"It was created for Charley. If a ladybug, a moth, even a nasty wasp got caught in the house, we had to capture it and set it free or she would cry. And when her friends fell and hurt themselves she would be there to comfort them with Band-Aids and Kool-Aid. She was steadfast, loyal and sweet, much like you. However, as she matured, she failed to develop one important quality: moxie. People and circumstances could hurt her easily, sometimes to the point where she couldn't rebound."

"And Emile Voorhees hurt her, didn't he?" I nearly choked on my words.

"She was crazy about him, God only knows why. But since they first met when she worked for him at Beauty by Design she thought she saw her chance for true love and happiness. He was good to her at first. He showered her with gifts and bought her special dinners. I didn't realize he was a married man, at first. Later on, after we found out, he gave her some song and dance about his marriage being on the rocks. It may have been true, but with him it was just an excuse, a lie, as I'm sure you found out." Art reached into his shirt pocket and pulled out a heart-shaped necklace with a marquis diamond in the middle.

"It's the design Voorhees gave to your daughter. I saw the picture on your desk. You had the necklace at the bar the night Emile died."

"I carry it with me every day to remind me of Charlene and what he did to her."

"And what he did to her from your perspective was kill her, indirectly, but still death was the outcome," I said. I hated to be so blunt, but whether Emile deserved life or death was not for Art to decide. Murder is murder.

"Emile was a conniving philanderer who only cared about himself and money. What goes around comes around," Art said.

I paused. "Art, did you try to scare me off the case by breaking into my shop and leaving me a threatening note?"

He went around the bar with his wine glass and poured himself another one. "Yes, you were getting too close for comfort. I heard you had a run-in with Taglianno and thought if you feared the Mafia was after you, you might stop questioning people. One night after work, I cut up some gourmet magazines and pieced together the threatening letter. I'm sorry; I never would have hurt you. I didn't expect you to be at your store. You scared me as much as I scared you, I'm sure."

"Probably so."

Art left the bar and walked toward the rear windows, wine glass still in hand. I followed. He cracked one of the French doors open a few inches. "I've always loved the view from here. Even in the darkness with the rain, you can still see it with your ears. The sound of the water hitting the shore and the night birds calling." He threw back the last ounce of wine left in his glass.

"Me too. This has always been the room with a view," I said.

"I know you don't have children yet," Art said. "Someday I hope you will. When you do, I think you'll look back on this and have a better understanding of my actions." His eyes glistened with tears. "When your children are little and they fall and skin their knees, you'll want to kiss them and make them better. When your daughter comes home in tears from her first high school dance because the boy she had a crush on danced with someone else, you'll want to hold her in your arms until the pain subsides." He walked over to a table and rested his palms on the edge. "And when she becomes an adult, and a hideous, lying man steals her virginity and her dignity . . ." He slammed his fist into the tabletop. "When your only child decides suicide is her only escape from a broken heart, well, I really had no choice, don't you see?"

I didn't have to lobby for a confession. It flowed like a broken dam gushing out in sorrowful waves of memory.

He collapsed into the nearby chair and wiped his upper lip with the back of his hand. "After my wife died in a car accident not long after Charlene's death, I felt I had no reason to go on. I needed a change. I thought moving here would be good for me. This place held happy memories of family vacations. I took the job here at the yacht club to help make ends meet. But, in my case, good wasn't going to last long. When I found out Emile Voorhees was a member, something snapped inside of me." He rubbed his hands together. "I became obsessed with thoughts of his death."

"Was the murder planned for that night?"

"No. I hadn't planned anything, but when I saw my office door open I peered in. There he was lying on my couch and the picture of my wife and Charlene had been moved. He knew who I was and yet he chose to lie down there and touch my things. It was like he was saying Charlene's suicide was no big deal. I flew into a rage. I went across the hall into the kitchen. All the help was up front. I picked up a knife that was lying near the dishwasher. I went back and peeked into my office again. Voorhees wasn't moving. I looked around, slipped in and plunged the chef's knife into his conniving back. Everyone in the kitchen including me had used the knife that night, so I didn't think much about fingerprints. It was finished. Besides, I didn't care if I got caught." He paused for a moment, staring out the window again. "I knew I wouldn't be able to hide the truth forever. You are one clever young lady."

"I have an instinct for these things," I said lamely. "My husband calls it women's intuition."

Art nodded and smiled and continued to tell his story. "It would have worked perfectly if only Susan hadn't interfered."

My heart skipped a beat. I could almost excuse a bereaving, if somewhat demented, father his revenge against a villain like Voorhees, but what had Susan done? How did she fit into this mix?

The chef answered my question before I could ask it. "Susan knew before anyone. She managed to put two and two together because of things Emile told her about Charlene during their relationship." He leaned over, put his elbows on his knees and cradled his head in his hands. "He couldn't even be a gentleman after they broke up."

I placed a hand on his shoulder and said, "Please go on."

"She called me to meet her at her boat after work the Friday night following the ball. I climbed aboard and we went below at first. She had been drinking alone and she offered me a glass. I declined and put it back inside the open cabinet. She was angry and had enough to drink for the two of us. She said she hadn't thought much of Emile lately, but at one time she had loved him and she wouldn't let me get away with murder. She told me she had seen me dangling Charlene's necklace when Emile was on the dance floor. Then to make matters worse she noticed me by my office not too long before the lights went out. She didn't think anything of it until she found Emile dead. Then she worried that the police might think she was guilty. She wanted me to confess. We argued and she tried to hit me. We struggled. I didn't mean to hurt her. Really. But she fell and hit her head on the winch. She was groggy but not dead. She pushed me away and told me to leave. I left her, I swear, alive. I should have called a doctor, but I was scared. I went home and waited for the police to show up at my door, but they never came. After I heard they found her body, I understood why."

Art stood, his face pale, his eyes fixed on me. "Don't you see I didn't have any choice? There's only one thing left to do now."

CHAPTER 26

Thunder clapped as Art's clenched fist reached out toward me. As I contemplated my early demise, he came closer, opening his hand. "I want to give you this." There lying curled in his palm was the necklace. If it had never existed, lives might have been saved.

"My daughter would have liked you to have this. It's far too pretty to throw away. I think we should call the police now." I wanted to tell Art the truth. He wasn't the real murderer, but under the circumstances I decided I would feel safer if the police were on the scene to back me up. I touched my brow in thanks for small—and in this case large—blessings. We started to head to the phone behind the bar when we both turned like synchronized swimmers toward the front door. In the heat of the moment I had almost forgotten about the one additional phone call I had made.

The true murderer faced us gun in hand. My mind raced. I thought about ducking under a table, but then what? All I could muster was a simple, "Hello, Gina. I wasn't certain until this moment if my phone call was to the right person."

"I didn't have much choice now, did I?" She motioned with her gun for Art and me to sit on two barstools. "You said you knew who the murderer was and if I wanted to keep my husband's name out of the papers, I'd better show up. Life has been very convenient for me the past few weeks, first with Emile the night of the ball and now tonight with the two of you. Too bad a burglar is going to break in here and murder you when you discover him."

Burglar? I got it. Gina planned to kill us and make the crime look like a break-in. I needed time. Time enough for Nick to show his handsome face and rescue us.

"Before the burglary begins, how about you let me explain to Art who Emile's real killer is?" I didn't wait for a response.

Art eyed me quizzically.

"You didn't kill him, Art," I said. "You may have wanted to, but when you stabbed him he was already dead. That's because someone else got to him first. Isn't that right, Gina?"

"Aren't you the clever one?" she said. "I should have seen it coming the day you came to visit. You caught me off guard. I just happened to be wearing the necklace Emile gave me. I saw you noticed it. You're a competent reporter, I'm sure you found out about them?"

"Actually, at the time I didn't notice. It wasn't until this evening it all came together. Emile's anagrams to thwart curious eyes, like 'It a Gang.' It's an anagram for 'Gina Tag' short for Gina Taglianno. Then I went over the conversation we had at your house. You said you knew the Voorheeses were new members, but when you and your husband met Nick and me here at the club, Tony said that neither of you knew the Voorheeses were members. That made me suspect you had some contact with him that your husband didn't know about—and it had nothing to do with jewelry deals. That, along with the heart-shaped necklace you were wearing when I visited you, the fact that you owned your own greenhouse to plant whatever you wanted added up to only one thing in my mind: murder. Why don't you share the details of how you poisoned him?" I knew I was making some assumptions, but the longer the discussion the better chance Art and I had of forestalling our own murders.

"Poison, yes. It seemed ladylike and untraceable. And it would have stayed that way if you hadn't interfered."

I rolled my eyes. "The lab results weren't conclusive as to the cause of death. They were still analyzing. You must have researched what you used pretty well."

"'Adopt the pace of nature; her secret is patience.' That's a quote from Ralph Waldo Emerson. I live by that credo. My secret is patience too. I cultivated and researched and waited. The Barbados nut, the belladonna plant, foxglove, lily of the valley—they can be formulated into a spectacularly lethal combination. Their action mimics a heart attack so, lucky me, the evidence pointed elsewhere. I knew Emile's favorite drink, Rèmy Martin on the rocks, same as my husbands. A little slight of hand when no one was at his table to exchange one poisoned drink with his and poof, the deed was done. Later, with the confusion of everything, I picked up their dishes and put them in the sink so all residue was washed away."

"But why?" Art exclaimed. "I couldn't stand the thought that I would have to see his face here on a regular basis, but you? What did you have to gain?"

"Gain? Nothing but everything because no one uses me and then casts me aside the way he did. Remember I learned from the very best. I married into the Taglianno family. You take what you want and never let your enemies get what they need. I found out he stole my husband's family jewels in the same month he broke off his affair with me. Then he had the gall to tell me to get Tony off his back or else he would tell him about our dalliance. No one threatens a Taglianno, no one." She brushed the hair from her forehead with the butt of the gun, and then pointed the weapon at Art. "Go behind the bar, open the cash register and slide the money over to me."

Art did as he was told. I sat stiff-kneed and motionless. I had run out of stalling tactics. I could throw a wine bottle, but my aim had never been that good. Just as I caught a sob escaping from my throat, the lights went off. I heard a distinct click-click across the floor. A shot rang out. There were sounds of heavy breathing, a whoosh and a thud. I screamed.

Before I knew what had happened the lights came back on. Gina lay prone on the floor, Cooper on top of her. "Are you all right?" Nick asked, looking me up and down with fear then scolding.

"I am now." Then without thinking I added, "What took you so blasted long?"

Nick shrugged. "There was this story I was telling Mrs. Chesney. Then I got your message on the refrigerator and I had to get a hold of Mark." He pointed toward Sherman who was standing by the light switch gun in hand. I gave them both the *look*.

"I know, I know," Nick said." My golf tales are always too long."

"Get this animal off me. Can't you see I'm hurt?" Gina Taglianno cried.

Sherman's shot had grazed her leg. She wasn't seriously wounded.

"I'll call 9-1-1," he said.

EPILOGUE

Wednesday, December 25

It was Christmas morning. The snow was falling like tiny bits of lace as early sun crept across the floorboards. Cooper lay at the bottom of the bed. He stared up at Nick and waited for one of us to stir. We knew better than to open an eyelid or utter a sound. Once we did we would have a hundred-pounds-plus of fur and fury on top of us and any hope of a few minutes of additional sleep would be lost. We squeezed hands under the sheets, but it was enough movement for Cooper gave warning. He barked a deep wolf bark and pounced.

Before long we were all out of bed donning slippers and bathrobes. I tied a new Christmas bandana around Cooper's neck. We marched down the hall in single file: Cooper first, then me and last Nick who put on a pot of coffee.

"I'll make us some sticky buns," I said.

"Straight from your mother's oven?"

"Eggs-actly." I grabbed a cellophane-covered plate we had received the previous night at my parents' house. My mother bakes the best sticky buns in the world, gooey icing and all. I promised myself one of these days I would learn to make them too. For now, however, Mom's handiwork would do fine. After a bit of warming in the microwave and a potty break for Cooper, we settled into the family room. The Christmas tree sparkled with tiny white lights and seashells I had collected from the shore the previous summer.

We plopped down on the couch with steaming mugs. "Congratulations again on the excellence in journalism award you got last week. It was well deserved," Nick said.

"Thanks. I hate to think it came at the expense of two deaths, Emile's and Susan's. But at least Frank and Carol seem to be taken with each other. I wonder if they're spending Christmas together."

"Not if his mother has anything to say about it. Let's just be thankful the killer's been caught and Art, once his probation's over with and he gets a bit of counseling, will be back to his jolly old self in no time. I do wish you'd stick to the job of pet storeowner instead of investigative reporter, though. It has a better ring to it. Now onto bigger and brighter things." Nick's eyes gleamed with a secret. "I think Santa left you a present on the tree. Go look."

I gave him a skeptical glare and wondered if I was going to get a woman's golf glove—his way of urging me to get out on the course more often. I laid my mug down and went over to the tree. I examined the gifts piled under the branches, a few marked for Nick, some for me, and some for Cooper.

"No, not *under* the tree. *On* the tree."

I looked up. Hanging from a green satin bow was a small box wrapped in gold. Smiling I released it and snuggled it close to my chest. Opening it at a snail's pace so has to savor the moment; I let the wrappings fall to the floor. The outside of the black onyx box bore a distinctive logo. I opened the hinged lid. Inside lay a diamond and emerald bracelet, the one I had so admired at Beauty by Design.

I rushed to hug Nick. "Oh, honey, how did you know?" Cooper barked and chased his tail in an endless circle.

Don't Miss the Next

A Paws For Love Mystery

Murder on the 16th Green

Morgan's journalistic prowess and investigative spirit are put to the test again when a dead contractor is found behind her parent's new construction golf course home and her dad becomes one of the prime suspects.

Keep watching my website for updates!

Helpful Pet Index

www.rispca.com
The oldest Humane Organization in Rhode Island.

www.petfinder.com
Adopt a new family member from one of thousands of adoption/humane groups across the country.

www.bestfriends.org ~~ www.nsalamerica.org
Find a pet at some of the largest no-kill shelters in the country.

Recipe From
Paws For Love

~Easy Treats~
Chapter 16

1 Small Box of Milk-Bone dog biscuits
*1 pound of Carob Chips

Melt carob in a double boiler over medium low heat. When completely melted, dip in one side only of the biscuit to thoroughly coat. Lay on wax paper to cool. Yum.

*Carob can be used as a non-toxic alternative to chocolate in dog treats, as the theobromine (similar to caffeine) in chocolate is toxic to most dogs.

Printed in the United States
148470LV00002B/82/P

9 781601 457912